SHADOWS
IN
THE
TWILIGHT

COMPANION NOVELS BY HENNING MANKELL

A Bridge to the Stars

When the Snow Fell

Journey to the End of the World

HENNING MANKELL

SHADOWS IN THE TWILIGHT

TRANSLATED FROM THE SWEDISH BY LAURIE THOMPSON

DELACORTE PRESS

Translation copyright © 2007 by Laurie Thompson
Cover art © 2011 by Ebur Sidar/Trevillion Images

All rights reserved. Published in the United States by Delacorte Press, an imprint of Random House Children's Books, a division of Random House, Inc., New York. Originally published in hardcover in Sweden as *Skuggorna vaxer i skymningen* by Henning Mankell, copyright © 1990 by Henning Mankell, by Rabén & Sjögren Bokförlag, Stockholm, in 1991. Published by agreement with Norstedts Agency. This translation was originally published in paperback in Great Britain by Andersen Press Limited, London, in 2007, and was subsequently published in hardcover in the United States by Delacorte Press in 2008.

Delacorte Press is a registered trademark and the colophon is a trademark of Random House, Inc.

Visit us on the Web! www.randomhouse.com/teens

Educators and librarians, for a variety of teaching tools, visit us at www.randomhouse.com/teachers

The Library of Congress has cataloged the hardcover edition of this work as follows:
Mankell, Henning.
[Skuggorna vaxer i skymningen. English.]
Shadows in the Twilight / Henning Mankell ; translated by Laurie Thompson.
p. cm.
Originally published: Stockholm : Rabén & Sjögren Bokförlag, 1991, under the title, *Skuggorna vaxer i skymningen*.
Summary: Continues the story of Joel, now nearly twelve, who lives with his father in a small town in Sweden in 1957, when Joel is run over by a bus and survives without a scratch, then sets out to do a good deed in gratitude for this miracle.
ISBN 978-0-385-73496-7 (trade) — ISBN 978-0-385-90490-2 (glb)
[1. Accidents—Fiction. 2. Miracles—Fiction. 3. Fathers and sons—Fiction. 4. Single-parent families—Fiction. 5. Secret societies—Fiction. 6. Sweden—History—20th century—Fiction.] I. Thompson, Laurie. II. Title.
PZ7.M31283Sha 2008
[Fic]—dc22
2007017146

ISBN 978-0-440-24043-3 (tr. pbk.)

Printed in the United States of America

10 9 8 7 6 5 4 3 2

Random House Children's Books supports the First Amendment and celebrates the right to read.

SHADOWS
IN
THE
TWILIGHT

— ONE —

I have another story to tell.

The story of what happened next, when summer was over. When the mosquitoes had stopped singing and the nights turned cold.

Autumn set in, and Joel Gustafson had other things to think about. He hardly ever went to his rock by the river, to gaze up at the sky.

It was as if the dog that had headed for its star no longer existed.

Or perhaps it had never existed? Had it all been a dream?

Joel didn't know. But in the end he decided it was all to do with the fact that he'd soon be twelve. After his twelfth birthday he'd be too big to sit on a rock and dream about a strange dog that might never have existed in the real world.

Reaching the age of twelve was a great event. It would mean there were only three years to go before his fifteenth birthday. Then he'd be able to ride a moped and watch films in the Community Center that children were not allowed to see. When you were fifteen you were more of a grown-up than a child.

These were the thoughts whirring around in Joel's head one afternoon in September 1957. It was a Sunday, and he'd set out on an expedition into the vast forest that surrounded the little northern Swedish town he lived in.

Joel had decided to test if it was possible to get lost on purpose. At the same time he had two other important questions to think through. One was whether it would have been an advantage to have been born a girl, and called Joella instead of Joel. The other was what he was going to do when he grew up.

Needless to say, he hadn't mentioned any of this to his dad, Samuel. He'd been curled up by the kitchen window, watching Samuel get shaved. As Samuel always cut himself while shaving, Joel had decided long ago that he would grow a beard when he grew up. Once, when he'd been alone in the house, he'd carefully drawn a black beard on his face, using the burnt end of a stick of wood from the stove. To find out what it felt like to have hair on his face, he'd also wrapped a fox fur round his cheeks. He'd decided that having a beard was better than repeatedly cutting his face with a razor. But he hoped his beard wouldn't smell like a fox.

When Samuel had finished shaving, he'd put on his best suit. Then Joel had knotted his tie for him.

Now Samuel was ready to pay a visit to Sara, who had a day off from her work as a waitress in the local bar.

Now he's going to say that he won't be late, Joel thought.

"I won't be late," said Samuel. "What are you going to do with yourself this afternoon?"

Joel had prepared an answer to that question in advance.

"I'm going to do a jigsaw puzzle," he said. "That big one with the Indian chief, Geronimo. The one with nine hundred and fifty-four pieces."

Samuel eyed him up and down thoughtfully.

"Why don't you go out to play?" he asked. "It's lovely weather."

"I want to complete the puzzle against the clock," said Joel. "I'm going to try to set a new record. It took me four hours last time. Now I'm going to do it in three."

Samuel nodded, and left. Joel waved to him through the window. Then he took out an old rucksack he kept under his bed and packed some sandwiches. He'd put the kettle on to boil while he was doing that, and when it was ready he made some tea and poured it into Samuel's red thermos flask.

Borrowing Samuel's thermos flask was a bit risky. If he broke it or lost it, Samuel would be angry. Joel would be forced to produce a lot of complicated explanations. But it was a risk he would have to take. You couldn't possibly set out on an expedition without a thermos flask.

Last of all he took his logbook from the case where the sailing ship *Celestine* was displayed, collecting dust. He closed his rucksack, pulled on his Wellingtons and put on his jacket. He cleared the stairs in three jumps—it had taken him four only six months before.

The sun was shining, but you could feel it was autumn. To get to the forest as quickly as possible, Joel decided that the Indian Chief Geronimo was lying in ambush with his warriors behind the Co-operative Society's warehouse. So he would have to proceed on horseback. He geed himself up, imagined that his boots were the newly shod hooves of a dappled pony, and set off across the street. The reddish brown goods wagons in the railway siding were rocks he could hide behind. Once he got that far, Geronimo and his braves would never be able to catch up with him. And just beyond there was the forest....

When he'd reached the trees he closed down the game. Nowadays he thought that his imagination was something he could turn on or off like a water tap. He went into the forest.

As the sun was already low in the sky, it seemed to be twilight in among the trees. The shadows were growing longer and longer among the thick trunks.

Then the path petered out. There was nothing but forest all around him.

Just one more step, Joel thought. If I take one more step the whole world will disappear.

He listened to the sighing of the wind.

Now he would practice getting lost. He would do something nobody had ever done before. He would prove that it wasn't only people who took a wrong turning who could get lost.

A crow suddenly flew up from a high branch. It made Joel jump, as if it had been perched just beside him. Then silence fell once more.

The crow had scared him. He took a quick pace backwards and made sure that the world was still there. He hung his rucksack on a projecting branch and then took ten paces in a straight line in front of him, in among the trees. Then ten more. When he turned round he could no longer see his rucksack. He closed his eyes and spun round and round to make himself dizzy and lose his sense of direction. When he opened his eyes, he had no idea which direction he ought to take. Now he was lost.

There wasn't a sound all around him. Only the sighing of the wind.

He suddenly wanted to pack it all in.

Pretending you could get lost on purpose was an impossible game. It was being childish, and somebody who would soon be twelve years old couldn't allow himself to indulge in such silliness.

It struck Joel that this might be the big difference. That he would no longer be able to make believe.

He located his rucksack and returned to the road. He thought more about whether it would have been better if he'd been born a girl instead of a boy. What would be best, a Joel or a Joella?

Boys were stronger. And the games they played were more fun than those played by girls. When they grew up they had more exciting jobs. Even so, he wasn't sure. What was really best? Having a beard that smelled like a fox fur? Or having breasts that bounced up and down inside your sweater? Giving birth to children, or making children? Tickling or being tickled?

He trudged home without being able to make up his mind. He kicked hard at a stone. It had not been a good Sunday. When he got home he would write in his logbook that it had been a very bad day. He had no desire to do the Geronimo puzzle either. He had no desire to do anything at all. And tomorrow he would have to go back to school.

He bit his tongue as hard as he could, to make the day even worse. There was nothing he hated more than not knowing what to do next.

Life was a long series of Nexts. He had worked that out already. The trick was to make sure that the next Next was better than the previous one. But everything had gone wrong today.

He opened the gate into the overgrown garden of the house where he lived.

There were lots of red berries on the rowan tree.

The sun was just setting behind the horizon on the other side of the river.

Nothing happens, Joel thought.

Nothing ever happens in this dump.

But he was wrong.

The next day, which was a Monday with fog and drizzle, something happened that Joel could never have imagined in his wildest dreams.

He would experience a Miracle.

— TWO —

The day couldn't have begun any better for Joel.

When his dad, Samuel, shook him by the shoulder shortly after seven o'clock, he'd been having a nightmare. He'd dreamt that he was on fire. Sizzling flames had been shooting out of his nostrils, just like a fire-spitting dragon. His fingers were blue, a bit like the welding flames he'd seen at the Highways Department workshops, where he used to have his skates sharpened in the winter. Being on fire didn't hurt. Even so, he had felt terrified and wanted nothing more than to wake up. It wasn't until Samuel touched his shoulder that the flames were extinguished. He gave a start and sat up in bed.

"What's the matter?" asked Samuel.

"I don't know," said Joel. "I was dreaming that I was on fire."

Samuel frowned. Joel knew his father didn't like him having nightmares. Perhaps it was because Samuel himself sometimes had bad dreams? Joel had often been woken up in the middle of the night by Samuel shouting and screaming in his sleep.

One of these days Joel would ask his father about his dreams. He'd noted that down on the last page of his logbook, where he had listed all the questions he didn't yet have an answer to.

But everything had been fine this morning. Joel felt very relieved when he realized he'd only been dreaming. The fire had never actually existed. He was usually in a bad mood when he woke up and had to get out of bed. The cork tiles on the floor were far too cold for his bare feet. And then he could never find his clothes. His socks were always inside out and his shirt buttons wouldn't fit into their holes. In Joel's opinion the people who made clothes for children were wicked. How else could you explain the fact that nothing went right when you were in a hurry to get dressed and it was freezing cold in the room?

But this morning everything went much more smoothly. And when he went to the kitchen he found two little boxes of pastilles by the side of his cup of hot chocolate.

"They're from Sara," said Samuel, who was busy combing his tousled hair in front of the cracked shaving mirror.

Two packs of pastilles when you've narrowly escaped burning to death? And on a Monday morning?

It seemed to Joel that he was in for a good day. And it became even better when he opened the little boxes and took out the enclosed picture cards: they were of two footballers he didn't have in his collection. Joel collected footballers. Nothing else. He sometimes hit the roof when he opened a pack of pastilles and found a picture of a wrestler. That was the worst thing that could happen to him. Flabby wrestlers who were always called Svensson. And their first name was nearly always Rune.

But this morning he had found two footballers at the same time.

"Call in at the bar on the way home from school," said Samuel as he put on his jacket. "Sara will be pleased to see you."

"Why has she given me them?" Joel asked.

"She likes you," said Samuel. "Surely you know that?"

He paused in the doorway and turned round.

"Don't forget to buy some potatoes," he said. "And milk."

"I won't," said Joel.

It was good to hear that Sara liked him. Even though she wasn't his mum. Of course, it wasn't as good as hearing his mother, Jenny, saying it. But Jenny didn't exist. She had disappeared. And as long as she didn't exist, until Samuel and Joel had found her, Sara was welcome to say that she liked him.

As usual, he dawdled for so long over his cup of hot chocolate that he would be forced to run in order to get to school on time. Miss Nederström didn't like pupils arriving late. If she was really angry, or if you had been late over and over again, she sometimes twisted your ear and it hurt so much that you had to struggle to hold back the tears. But she only did that to boys. She didn't bother about girls turning up late. That was why Joel sometimes asked himself if it would have been better to be a girl called Joella Gustafson.

He put on his outdoor clothes, slung his satchel over his shoulder, locked the door and hid the key under Samuel's boots on the landing. He almost cleared the stairs in two-and-a-half jumps and sped off in the direction of school. He had three possible routes to choose from. Today he chose the one along Blixtens Road. He only went that way when he was very late. It was straight and dull, and only involved one shortcut, over the court-yard behind the chemist's. But it was the shortest route.

He ran as fast as he could, and arrived dead on time. Miss Nederström was just about to close the door when he came racing up.

"Good for you, Joel," she said. "I'm glad to see that you are making an effort to arrive on time."

School finished at two o'clock. Joel felt pleased with himself. He hadn't been asked any questions that he couldn't answer. And moreover, they'd had geography, which was the subject he liked best. He liked it just as much as he hated maths. He hadn't a clue about numbers.

It was the same story as with children's clothes. Who-ever invented numbers must have been a wicked person.

But the best part of the day was when Miss Nederström was angry with Otto because he hadn't been paying attention during a class. Joel didn't like Otto. Otto was his sworn enemy. He was at the very top of the list of people Joel hoped would always be in trouble. Otto was having to repeat a year, and never missed an opportunity to annoy people. To make matters worse, he was so strong that Joel couldn't get the better of him in the winter snowball fights.

Joel had suddenly had an idea during the geography lesson.

He would invent a geography game. He wasn't quite sure how it would work, but it would involve dice and a race to see who could travel round the world fastest. He was in a hurry to get home and start working on the game. He had a collection of old maps that he could cut up or draw on.

He very nearly forgot that he had to buy some potatoes and milk. But he was in luck again when he got to Ljunggren's Grocery Store: he was the only customer in the shop and didn't need to wait. Then he forgot that he'd promised to call in at the bar and thank Sara for the pastilles. He was almost home before he remembered.

His first reaction was not to bother—he could just as well thank her tomorrow.

But then he changed his mind. She had given him not just one box of pastilles, but two, after all. He turned round and retraced his steps.

And that was when the Miracle happened.

He didn't look both ways before running across the street. There was a cement mixer roaring and rattling away outside the ironmonger's, and a lorry was sounding its horn over by the bookshop.

He suddenly found himself bang in front of a big bus. Perhaps he heard the driver's frantic braking? Perhaps he didn't hear anything? But just as he was about to be crushed by one of the enormous wheels he slipped and fell over backwards. The bus drove over the top of him and crashed into a lamppost outside the bar.

Joel lay perfectly still. He could smell the oil and feel the heat from the bus's exhaust pipe that was coiled like a dirty steel snake a few centimeters away from his face.

It had all happened so quickly that he hadn't even had time to feel frightened.

As he lay there under the bus, he didn't understand what had happened.

Why was he lying there? And what was this thing above his face?

He turned his head to one side and saw feet moving backwards and forwards. A drop of oil hit him just below one eye. Somewhere out there he could hear voices shouting and screaming.

He heard somebody shouting that a child had been run over by the bus.

Was it him?

If it was him, why wasn't he dead?

He wasn't dead, surely? Everything was as usual, except that he was lying on his back on the wet street, and oil was dripping onto his face.

There must surely be a difference between being alive and being dead?

Then he felt somebody taking hold of his arm. A face edged its way closer to him. He recognized it. It was Nyberg's face. Nyberg was the bouncer in the bar where Sara worked.

"Are you all right, milad?" said the face. "For Christ's sake, I do believe you're alive."

"Yes," said Joel. "I think so."

That was the moment he started to feel frightened, and it slowly dawned on him that he had experienced a Miracle.

A bus had run him over. But at precisely the right moment he'd slipped and landed between the wheels. In addition the satchel with his school things and the milk and the potatoes had slid down by his side. If it had stayed on his back, his face would have been hit by the bus's chassis.

The Ljusdal bus, he thought. It had to be the bus to Ljusdal.

The Ljusdal bus had presented him with his Miracle.

He closed his eyes. Hands began to take hold of him, carefully, as if he were dead after all. Voices were whispering and shouting on all sides. He felt himself being dragged over the wet asphalt. Then somebody lifted him up onto a bed that was swaying back and forth. Metal doors closed and an engine started turning.

Somebody was sitting beside him, holding his hand.

He looked cautiously, hardly opening his eyes. He'd often practiced that in front of Samuel's shaving mirror. Looking in such a way that nobody could see he was looking.

The woman holding his hand was Eulalia Mörker, who ran a hairdressing business next to the ironmonger's. Eulalia spoke with a foreign accent and chased away children when they were too noisy outside her shop door. She would come running out brandishing a pair of curling tongs, shouting and threatening, and everybody was a bit scared of her, because you could never be sure what she was saying in her peculiar language.

Now she was sitting beside Joel, holding his hand.

Joel looked again, to make certain his eyes hadn't deceived him.

He turned his head slowly to see what sort of a car it was he was traveling in.

An ambulance. The only vehicle with a bed.

When he was transferred onto another stretcher at the hospital, he thought it would be best if he groaned. Not a lot, just a little one. Perhaps it wasn't a good idea to let people know too quickly that he'd experienced a Miracle.

He was examined by Dr. Stenström. Joel didn't like it when the nurses took off all his clothes. He was especially worried about them discovering that he had a large hole in his underpants. And he wasn't sure that his feet were properly clean. Somebody who had just experienced a Miracle maybe ought to have just got out of the bath?

Then he heard Stenström's authoritative voice.

"This young boy has been incredibly lucky," he said. "He's fallen under a bus but hasn't got a single scratch. It can only be described as a miracle."

A Miracle!

It was true. Dr. Stenström had realized.

Joel opened his eyes.

A bright light was shining down on him. There was something smelly stuck up his nose. The lamp was as hot as the sun. He could make out faces gathered round him, looking like white shadows, staring at him.

He suddenly thought about Jesus walking on water. That was Miss Nederström's favorite Bible story. He had no idea how many times she'd read it for them, but often enough for him to recall it almost by heart.

What had the people on the shore shouted when Jesus walked over the waves?

What was that long, difficult, incomprehensible word?

"Hallelujah!" he shouted when he remembered what it was.

"You can say that again," said Dr. Stenström. "Let's see if you can stand up."

A nurse helped him up. He sat on the examination table, dangling his legs. He could see his underpants on a chair, with the big hole in them.

Then he jumped down onto the floor.

"Not a scratch," said Dr. Stenström. "Guess who's going to be overjoyed."

"My dad, Samuel," said Joel, who thought he'd been asked a question.

"I'm sure he will be," said Dr. Stenström, "but I bet the bus driver is at least as glad."

Joel made as if to start getting dressed.

"We'll keep you in overnight," said Dr. Stenström. "Just to be on the safe side."

"I have to go home and prepare some potatoes," said Joel. "My dad will wonder what's going on if I don't."

"He's on his way here," said one of the nurses. Joel suddenly recognized her voice. She was the mother of one of his classmates. Eva-Lisa, who could run faster than anybody else in the class. She was like a greyhound.

Joel lay down on the examination table again.

All he wanted just now was to be left in peace. He still wasn't quite sure what had happened.

As if everybody in the room had read his mind, they all left. He quickly jumped down and hid his underpants beneath his shirt, so that the hole couldn't be seen. Then he checked to see if his feet were clean.

They weren't. He took some balls of cotton wool from a glass dish and poured onto them some liquid with a strong smell from out of a brown bottle. Then he rubbed his feet until they were clean. He had only just crept back under the blanket on the examination table when the door opened.

It was the bus driver.

Joel recognized him. His name was Eklund, and a year or two ago he had shot a bear. He was always the one who drove the Ljusdal bus.

"Well, milad," he said. "If only you knew. If only you knew how pleased I am."

"I wasn't looking where I was going," said Joel. "I hope the bus isn't broken."

"Who cares about the bus," said Eklund, wiping his runny nose with the back of his big red hand.

Joel could see that his eyes were red.

"I didn't have time to brake," Eklund said. "All of a sudden, there you were in front of the bus. I never thought you would survive. Never."

"I think it was a Miracle," said Joel.

Eklund nodded.

"I'll have to start going to church again," he said. "Hell's bells, I'll have to start going to church again."

The door opened once more. It was the Greyhound's mum who had come back again.

"The boy's father has just arrived," she said. "You'll have to go now. As you can see, there's nothing wrong with the lad."

"Thank God for that," said Eklund.

"Make sure you keep a better lookout in future," said the Greyhound's mum. "You bus drivers think you can drive as if you had the roads to yourselves!"

"I never drive too fast," said Eklund.

Joel could tell that Eklund was angry.

"We all have our own ideas about that," said the Greyhound's mum, shooing him out as if he'd been a cat intruding where he'd no business to be.

Then Samuel came into the room.

Joel thought it was best to give the appearance of being as wretched as possible.

Samuel's face was as white as a sheet. He was breathing heavily, as if he'd run all the way from the forest to the hospital.

He sat down on the edge of the bed, and looked at Joel.

Joel kept his eyes closed.

There wasn't a sound in the room.

Another kind of silence, Joel thought. Not the same as in the forest yesterday. Not like it is when I wake up in the middle of the night. Or when we're intent on putting Miss Nederström on the spot.

An entirely new kind of silence.

A Miracle silence.

"The potatoes are in my rucksack," said Joel. "But the milk bottle broke."

He suddenly felt frightened. He was scared stiff, in fact.

He thought about the broken milk bottle. The shards of glass and the white milk running out.

It could have been him.

The bottle of milk could easily have been his body that was crushed into a thousand pieces. The white milk could have been his blood.

He felt unable to move a muscle.

Now the penny dropped, and he realized what a narrow escape he'd had. He ought to be dead. But instead he was lying here on the examination table under the white blanket, and he hadn't suffered a single scratch.

But even though he hadn't been injured, he started to feel the pain.

It was a totally silent pain.

He closed his eyes, and heard the Greyhound's mum enter the room.

"The boy's tired," she said in a low voice.

"Is it absolutely sure that he hasn't been injured?" Samuel asked.

"Dr. Stenström is certain about that," said the Greyhound's mum. "But naturally, he had a bit of a scare. That's why we're keeping him in overnight for observation."

Joel felt himself being lifted from the examination table onto a trolley.

He peered through half-closed eyes and noted that he was being wheeled down a corridor. A door opened, and he was transferred into a bed.

"Can I stay here with him?" he heard his dad asking.

"Of course," said the Greyhound's mum. "Ring the bell if there's anything you want."

A Miracle, Joel thought.

Jesus walked on water. And I was run over by a Ljusdal bus but escaped without a single scratch.

He half-opened his eyes again.

Samuel was sitting on a chair by the window.

Joel knew what he was thinking about.

Jenny. His mum, Jenny, who'd simply vanished carrying a suitcase, and left them to get by on their own.

Joel knew that Samuel thought about her every time something unusual or unexpected happened. His dad might be sitting on the kitchen bench, or on the edge of Joel's bed, but he just stared into space. Joel would try to think the same thoughts as his father. Sometimes he had the feeling that he succeeded. But not always.

And now he was much too tired. Despite the fact that it was only afternoon. He could make out the sun through the window. The shadows were lengthening in the room, and he knew that twilight was falling.

Joel fell asleep, and didn't wake up until next morning.

Samuel stayed at the hospital all night. He didn't go to work in the forest. They drove home in a black taxi.

"Shouldn't I go to school?" asked Joel.

"Not today. Tomorrow," said Samuel.

"Shouldn't you go to work in the forest?"

"Not today. Tomorrow. Here we are, we're at home now."

Joel went to his room.

This was where he lived. He would continue to live here, even though he'd experienced a Miracle.

Samuel made him a pork pancake. It got burnt, but Joel didn't complain.

"What's a Miracle?" he asked.

Samuel seemed surprised by the question.

"You'll have to ask the vicar about that."

"But I was run over by a bus? And I didn't suffer a single scratch?"

"You were lucky," said Samuel. "Incredibly lucky. It's only people who believe in divine powers that talk about miracles."

Joel didn't bother to ask any more questions. He could tell from Samuel's tone of voice that his dad preferred not to talk about Miracles.

Joel knew that his father didn't believe in God. Once when Samuel had been drunk, he'd hurled a bucket at the wall and cursed and shouted that there were no such things as gods. If Miss Nederström was right, that meant that Samuel was a lost soul.

Mind you, Joel had no idea what a lost soul was.

But he realized that he would have to give serious thought to what he believed in connection with God, now that the Ljusdal bus had enabled him to experience a Miracle.

After dinner, when Samuel had fallen asleep on the kitchen bench, Joel took his logbook out of the showcase containing the *Celestine*. On the last page, where he used to list all his unanswered questions, there was hardly any space left. There was only just enough room for one word and a question mark.

"*God?*"

If you had experienced a Miracle, you ought to thank God for it.

But if Joel was in the same category as Samuel, a lost soul, how should he go about that?

How do you thank a God that you might not believe in?

And what would happen if you didn't say thank you?

Would the Miracle be withdrawn, so that you would be run over by the Ljusdal bus again?

Joel sighed. There were too many questions. And the questions were too big. He wished there was one day every week when all questions were banned.

He replaced his logbook, went to his room and started to cut up an old map he had. Now he would start inventing his new Around the World game.

Samuel had woken up and suddenly appeared in the doorway.

"What are you doing?" he asked.

"Making a game," said Joel.

"You're not sitting here and thinking about the accident, I hope?"

"It wasn't an accident."

"What was it, then?"

"I didn't get a single scratch. So it can't have been an accident, can it?"

Samuel looked as if he didn't know what to say.

"You must try to stop thinking about it," he said. "If you have nightmares, wake me up."

Samuel went to his room and switched on the radio. The evening news program was on. Joel stood in the doorway. Perhaps they would say something about the Miracle that had taken place.

But there was no mention of it.

No doubt the Miracle was too small to report.

The next day he went to school as usual. He avoided going past the bar and seeing the damaged lamppost. He was also a little bit worried that the bus might come back and run him over again.

He must find a way of saying thank you for the Miracle.

And he must do so quickly.

When he got to school Miss Nederström gave him a hug.

That had never happened before.

She squeezed him so hard that he had difficulty in breathing.

She used a very strong-smelling perfume and Joel didn't like being hugged at all. His classmates looked very solemn, and Joel had the feeling that they were afraid of him, as if he were a ghost. A walking phantom.

It was both good and bad.

It was good that everybody was paying attention to him. But it was bad that he had to be a ghost for that to happen.

Things weren't made any better when Miss Nederström told him that he should thank God for having survived.

I hope she doesn't ask me to do that here in the classroom, Joel thought.

I'm not going to do that.

But she left him in peace. He could start breathing again.

It was hard to concentrate on the lessons. And in the breaks it seemed as if his classmates were avoiding him. Even Otto left him alone.

Joel didn't like all this at all.

If people thought he had a contagious disease just because a Miracle had happened to him, he'd rather it hadn't done.

It was all that confounded Eklund's fault, of course, the man with the big red hands who hadn't been driving carefully. If you were driving a bus you had to expect somebody to run over the road because he was in a hurry to say thank you for two packs of pastilles. Didn't they teach bus drivers anything before giving them their driving licenses?

After school Joel trudged back home.

He would have to find a good way of saying thank you for the Miracle.

And he would have to be quick about it.

No doubt there was an aura around him telling everybody that he still hadn't said thank you to God.

Feeling in a bad mood, he went down to the river and sat down on his rock.

He felt he had to talk to somebody about this Miracle.

Not Samuel. That wouldn't be any good. His father didn't like people talking about God.

Who should he talk to, then?

The Old Bricklayer, Simon Windstorm?

Or Gertrud, who lived on the other side of the river and didn't have a nose?

It occurred to him that he didn't have a real friend. A best friend.

That was something he'd have to get.

That was the most important of all the things he'd have to solve this autumn.

You couldn't celebrate your twelfth birthday without having a real friend.

He made up his mind to pay a visit to Gertrud No-Nose that very same evening.

He left his rock, went home and put the potatoes on to boil.

When Samuel had finished his dinner, it was time for Joel to tell him that he was going out. He had prepared for this carefully.

"I'm going to call on Eva-Lisa for a bit," he said.

Samuel put down the newspaper he'd been reading.

"Who?" he said.

"Eva-Lisa."

"Who's she?"

"Come on, you must know. She's in my class. Her mum's that nurse at the hospital. The one you met."

"Oh, her," said Samuel. "But shouldn't you stay at home tonight?"

"But I don't have a single scratch!"

Samuel nodded. Then he smiled.

"Don't be late, then," he said. "And make sure you stick to the pavements."

"I will, don't worry," said Joel. "I shan't be late. Just a couple of hours."

A few minutes later he was hurrying over the river. The arch of the bridge towered over his head.

He remembered clinging on to the very top of it, when Samuel had come to help him down. He ran over the bridge as fast as he could.

He was forced to pause outside Gertrud's gate and get his breath back. The cold autumn wind was tearing at his chest.

Maybe Gertrud could help him to find a good way of saying thank you for the Miracle, and getting quits with God, or whoever it was that prevented the Ljusdal bus from killing him.

He opened her squeaky gate.

He glanced up at the starry sky. But there was no sign of the dog.

— THREE —

There was only one thing Joel could be certain about as far as Gertrud was concerned. That she didn't have a nose.

But that was all. Gertrud had lost her nose as a result of an operation that went wrong, and Joel couldn't make her out. Nearly everything she did was Contrary. Although she attended the Pentecostal chapel where the minister was known as Happy Harry, she didn't look like the other ladies in his congregation. They all dressed in black and wore flat hats with a little black net over their faces. They wore galoshes and carried brown handbags. But Gertrud didn't. Never. She made her own clothes. Joel had spent several evenings in her kitchen, watching her at work on her sewing machine. She made new clothes out of old ones. She sometimes cut two old coats down the middle, then sewed them together to make a new one. Joel used to help her to pin the seams. She never had a proper hat, although she often wore an old army fur cap pulled down over her ears. Once upon a time it had been yellowish white, but Gertrud liked bright colors and had dyed it red.

Joel thought that Gertrud was a difficult person. He could never be sure what she was going to do or say. That could be exciting, but also annoying. She sometimes wanted Joel to accompany her on some frolic or other, and made him feel embarrassed. But at other times he thought she was the most fascinating person in the whole world.

Gertrud was grown up. Nearly thirty. Three times as old as Joel. Even so, she could act like a child on occasions. Like a child even younger than Joel.

She was a grown-up childperson. And that could be difficult to cope with.

Joel stood outside the kitchen door and listened. Sometimes Gertrud was feeling sad, and would sit sobbing on a chair in the kitchen. She had a special Weeping Chair in the corner next to the cooker. She seemed to have arranged a punishment corner for herself.

Joel didn't like it when Gertrud was crying. She sobbed far too loudly. It wasn't as if she had a stomachache, or had fallen and hit herself, but it sounded as if she were in pain.

In Joel's view, when you were feeling sad you should cry quietly. You should cry so quietly that nobody could hear you. Not bawl your head off and bring the world to a standstill. You could do that if you were in pain, but not just because you were sad.

On several occasions Joel had run over the bridge to pay a visit to Gertrud, only to find her sobbing in the kitchen. So he had turned and gone back home again.

But now there wasn't a sound to be heard from the kitchen.

Joel pressed his ear against the cold door and listened hard.

Then he pulled a string hanging next to the door.

Immediately, lots of bells started playing a tune.

That was what Joel liked most about Gertrud. Nothing in her house was usual. She didn't even have a normal doorbell with a button to press. Instead, she had a string to pull, and that set off lots of bells, like a musical box.

Gertrud had invented it herself. She had taken an old wall clock to pieces and attached to the parts several little bells she'd bought from Mr. Under, the horse dealer— the kind that ring when his horses pull sleighs through the snow. And she'd made the contraption work.

The rest of her house was the same.

Once he had been helping Gertrud to do an uninspiring jigsaw puzzle on the kitchen table when she suddenly jumped to her feet and brushed all the pieces onto the floor. They'd almost finished the puzzle; there were only a few pieces left.

"I have an idea!" Gertrud had shouted.

"Aren't we going to finish the puzzle?" Joel had asked.

Even as he spoke he realized what a silly question that was. All the pieces were scattered over the cork floor tiles. If they were going to finish the puzzle, they'd have to start all over again.

Gertrud put a red clown's nose over the hole beneath her eyes. She usually had a handkerchief stuffed into the hole where her nose had been, but when she was going to think, or when she was in a good mood, she would put on the red nose.

She used to call it her Thinking Nose.

"Never mind the puzzle," Gertrud exclaimed. "We're going to do something else."

"What?" wondered Joel.

Gertrud didn't answer, but looked mysterious.

Then she opened a wardrobe and pulled out lots of clothes in a heap on the floor.

"We're going to change," she said.

Joel didn't know what she was talking about.

"Change?" he asked. "Change what?"

"Everything that's normal or usual!" shouted Gertrud. "Everything that's usual and boring."

Joel still didn't understand what she was talking about. And so he didn't know if what was going to happen would be exciting, or if he would be embarrassed.

"Let's get dressed up," said Gertrud, and started sorting through the pile of clothes. "Let's start by changing ourselves."

Joel was all for that.

He liked dressing up. When he came home from school and was waiting for the potatoes to boil, he would often try on some of his father's clothes. A few years ago it had just been a game, but this last year Joel had been dressing up in Samuel's clothes to find out what it was like to be grown up. And he had discovered that although, obviously, clothes for adults were bigger than clothes for children, that was not the only difference. Lots of other things were different. For instance, clothes for adults had special pockets that children didn't need. Pockets to keep a watch in. Or a little pocket inside an ordinary pocket where you could keep small change.

Joel had noticed that he started thinking in a different way when he was wearing Samuel's clothes. He sometimes looked into the mirror and spoke to his reflection as if he had been his own father. He would ask the reflection how he'd got on at school, and if he'd remembered to call in at the baker's and buy some bread. The reflection never answered. But Joel used to take an invisible watch from the appropriate pocket, sigh deeply and urge the reflection not to forget the next day.

He had once discovered a dress right at the back of Samuel's wardrobe. It was hanging in a special bag that smelled of mothballs. Joel assumed it was one that Mummy Jenny had forgotten when she walked out on them. Who else could it belong to? Sara, the waitress in the local bar, was much too fat to get into it. Besides, she never stayed the night when she came to visit.

Joel had forbidden it.

He hadn't actually said anything. But he had forbidden it even so.

He had thought it so intensively that Sara had no doubt been able to read his thoughts.

So it must be his mum's dress.

But was it absolutely certain that she'd forgotten it when she packed her suitcase and left?

Had she left it behind on purpose?

So that it would be there if ever she came back?

Joel had taken it carefully out of the bag. It was blue and had a belt attached to the waist.

He had spent ages staring at the dress as it lay on the kitchen table. He'd looked at it for so long that the potatoes had boiled dry in the saucepan. He only stopped staring at the dress when the kitchen started filling with smelly smoke from the burnt potatoes.

He put it back into the wardrobe.

But a few days later he took it out again. This time, he tried it on.

He had the feeling that he'd never been as close to Mummy Jenny as at that moment.

He stood on a chair in front of the cracked shaving mirror, so that he could see the belt round his waist.

Then he returned the dress to the wardrobe.

He'd never been able to make up his mind whether his mum had forgotten it, or left it behind on purpose.

But he couldn't think about that now. Gertrud was

wading around through all the clothes scattered over the floor.

"Put these on," said Gertrud, handing him a pair of yellow trousers. "Hurry up! After eight o'clock in the evening it's too late to change what's usual."

"Why?" Joel wondered.

"It just is," said Gertrud. "Hurry up, now!"

Joel put on the trousers. They were far too long for him. He recalled that Gertrud had once made them from a few old curtains. Then he put on a checked shirt, and Gertrud knotted a tie round his neck, just like Joel used to do for his father. Gertrud was wearing an old pair of overalls that used to belong to the Fire Brigade. Joel had once asked her how she managed to come by so many old clothes.

"That's my secret," she'd replied. "I suppose you know what a secret is?"

Joel knew.

A secret was something you kept to yourself.

The house where Gertrud lived had three rooms. It was a normal house, with nothing peculiar about it. But what was different was that it had two kitchens. Joel didn't know anybody at all who had two kitchens, apart from Gertrud.

The other kitchen, the small one, was in Gertrud's bedroom, along one wall. There was an electric hot plate and a little sink with hot and cold water.

"Why do you have two kitchens?" Joel had asked, the first time he'd seen it.

"Because I'm so lazy," Gertrud had said. "In the mornings when I wake up, I don't have the strength to go as far as the big kitchen. So I make myself some coffee in here."

That made Joel suspect that Gertrud wasn't all there. But as there was nothing dangerous or frightening about her way of being different, he'd decided that it was just exciting.

Exciting and strange.

He had even gone so far as to invent a word to describe Gertrud. None of the words he knew was good enough, and so he'd joined together *exciting* and *strange* to make a new word.

Gertrud was *strangeiting*.

But he'd never told her that. Perhaps it was forbidden to invent new words? Perhaps there was a committee of stern-faced old men in gray suits somewhere or other, deciding what words could exist and which ones were forbidden?

Joel even had a secret word for forbidden words.

He called them *unwords*.

Gertrud dragged him over to the mirror in the middle room. It was the biggest of the three rooms. It was also the most fascinating one. There were so many things in it that it was almost impossible to pick your way through it. There was a big birdcage hanging from the ceiling. But Gertrud kept a stuffed hare inside it. There was an aquarium next to one of the walls. A lamp attached to the side of it lit it up—but there were no fish swimming around in the warm water. Instead, there was a toy locomotive on the sandy bottom. A big sofa in the middle of the floor was crammed full of books. Hanging on the walls were carpets like the ones Joel was used to seeing on the floor. But Gertrud's floor was made up of piles of sand and stones, and sometimes in the winter she would cover it in fir branches brought in from the forest.

There was a big mirror in one corner of the room. They stood in front of it, and laughed at each other.

"Good," said Gertrud. "Now we're not usual any longer. So we can begin."

Joel looked at her in surprise. To be honest, he felt a bit odd in the yellow trousers and the checked shirt. There again, he couldn't help being curious to know what she was going to think of next.

Gertrud sat down on the floor, and Joel followed suit.

"Just look at that," she said.

"Look at what?" Joel wondered.

Gertrud pointed at a lamp dangling on a cord hanging from the ceiling.

"Just look at that lamp," she said. "It looks so usual. A normal lamp hanging on a normal cord from a normal ceiling. We'll have to do something about that. What can we turn it into?"

"I don't know," said Joel. "I mean, a lamp is a lamp?"

"But it doesn't have to look normal," said Gertrud. "Just think if it looked like a mushroom instead!"

"A mushroom?" said Joel.

"You must know what a mushroom is? Now you'll find out what a mushroomlamp looks like."

"A mushroom," said Joel.

Gertrud laughed and nodded.

Joel watched her disconnect the plug, which was high up on one of the walls, and take down the lamp. She was balancing precariously on the pile of books on the big sofa. Then she fetched a broken broom handle from the closet, and fixed it in an old Christmas tree stand. She produced some tape and fastened the bulb to the top of the broom handle, and covered it with an old lampshade. She found some yellow fabric in the pile of clothes on the floor, and spread it carefully over the lampshade. Then she reconnected the plug.

To his surprise, Joel had to admit that the lamp really did look like a mushroom.

Now the penny had dropped. He joined in on the fun as well. He transformed the radiator under one of the windows into a tiger. He painted stripes onto it, and gave it a tail. He turned a wastepaper basket into a car by attaching to it a circle of bent wire to make a steering wheel. Meanwhile, Gertrud was busy turning a heavy chest of drawers into a sailing boat.

Then they sat down on the floor to get their breath back.

"That's better," said Gertrud, sounding very pleased

with herself. "But we really ought to redecorate this room. Maybe we ought to board up the windows and paint new windows on the walls."

"But you wouldn't be able to air the room then," said Joel.

"Maybe not," said Gertrud. "But only maybe. Perhaps we could do it even so?"

It seemed to Joel that when you thought about it, what Gertrud was doing was no more chaotic than things sometimes were back home with Samuel. The only difference was that Gertrud never bothered to tidy up. As far as she was concerned, there was no such thing as untidiness.

All these were thoughts flashing through Joel's mind as the bells were ringing after he'd pulled the string outside Gertrud's door.

In just a few seconds, he'd managed to think about what had taken several hours to happen in reality.

That was one of the unanswered questions he'd noted down on the last page of his logbook.

How could you remember things so quickly?

He tugged at the string again.

Gertrud went to prayer meetings at her church in the evening. She also used to work her way through the town, knocking on doors and trying to sell a religious magazine. She had told Joel that this was how she earned her living. And he'd heard other people say that Gertrud No-Nose was very poor.

But she's not poor, Joel thought.

If she didn't have any money, she would have no trouble inventing ways of making some.

Eventually he heard her shuffling up to the door in her slippers.

He quickly changed his face so that he looked like somebody who had just experienced a Miracle.

The door opened, and there was Gertrud.

Her face was bright blue. As blue as the bluest of summer skies.

"Joel!" she exclaimed.

Then she pulled him into the porch and flung her arms around him.

Joel noticed that his face turned blue as well.

That's torn it, he thought angrily.

There aren't any blue people who have experienced a Miracle. There aren't any blue people at all, full stop.

Gertrud looked solemnly at him.

"I've heard what happened," she said. "Thank God things turned out all right."

She ushered him into the kitchen, where it was very warm. The old wood-burning stove was crackling away.

On the kitchen table was a large dish full of blue paint.

"What are you doing?" Joel asked.

"I'd intended painting that white china tea service," said Gertrud. "But it was so boring that I decided to paint myself instead."

Joel took off his hat and unbuttoned his jacket. He

could see in the little mirror on the kitchen table that his nose and one cheek were blue.

He looked at Gertrud, at her blue face. Even the handkerchief stuffed into the hole where her nose should be was blue.

He suddenly felt very annoyed by the obvious fact that she was out of her mind.

She ought to have realized that he would come to see her when he had just experienced a Miracle.

In which case she could have avoided painting herself blue!

She sat down opposite him and eyed him solemnly.

"I was so frightened when I heard what had happened," she said. "I nearly had a heart attack! Just think if you'd been killed, and I never saw you again, Joel."

Joel felt a lump in his throat. He was forced to bite the inside of his lip to prevent himself from bursting into tears.

He tried to think of something else. Of the rucksack he'd hung from a branch in the forest. That Sunday afternoon, when he'd abandoned the big Geronimo puzzle and gone out into the forest instead, to prove that you could get lost on purpose.

That seemed so long ago! Such an incredibly long time ago!

Gertrud still looked very serious. It struck Joel that it was very odd for a person with a blue face to look so serious.

And especially Gertrud! Mad Gertrud!

"It must have been a Miracle," said Joel. "What else could it be?"

"God performs miracles," said Gertrud. "He performed one for me."

Joel knew what she meant. Gertrud had once tried to commit suicide. It was just after her operation had gone wrong and she'd lost her nose. She didn't think she could live without a nose. She would be too ugly to face up to life. She had filled her pockets with old-fashioned heavy irons, and jumped into the freezing cold river. But she hadn't drowned. She had got stuck in an uprooted tree in such a way that her head was above the water. Nor had she frozen to death. Mr. Under, the horse dealer, had been walking along the riverbank looking for a horse that had escaped from a paddock. He saw her face and thought it was the horse that had fallen into the water. He ran to fetch a rowing boat, pulled her out, and she survived.

She'd told all that to Joel herself. Not so very long ago. One evening they'd been building an igloo out of white sheets in the middle room, and telling each other True Stories. Joel had told her about Mummy Jenny, who'd gone away and left Joel and Samuel on their own. And Gertrud had told him about the time when she threw herself into the river.

That's good, Joel thought. She knows what a Miracle is.

"What do you do?" he asked.

"Do?"

"When you've been on the receiving end of a Miracle? Do you have to say thank you?"

Gertrud smiled.

"You don't have to say thank you," she said. "But you can be grateful."

Joel wasn't satisfied by that answer.

"I don't want the Miracle to be reversed," he said. "I don't want to be run over by the Ljusdal bus again."

Gertrud eyed him thoughtfully.

"Do you believe in God?" she asked. "Like I do?"

Joel shrugged.

"I don't know. I suppose I'm the same as Samuel."

"What's he, then?"

"A lost soul."

Gertrud burst out laughing. She laughed so much that the blue paint ran down her face and onto her white blouse.

"Who said that?" she asked. "Who said your dad is a lost soul?"

Joel shrugged again. He always did that when he wasn't sure what to say.

"Miss Nederström is always talking about lost souls," he mumbled.

Gertrud shook her head.

"God's not like that," she said. "But if you want to show that you are grateful for the miracle, you can do a good deed."

That was it! Of course! He would do a good deed. Why hadn't he thought of that himself? He'd read about it in books. People who had been in great danger but survived expressed their gratitude by doing a good deed.

Now he knew.

He nodded to Gertrud.

"I'll think of something," he said. "I shall do a good deed."

Gertrud suddenly looked sad.

That was probably the hardest thing about Gertrud to cope with, the fact that she was always changing her mood. Joel could also become angry or sad very quickly, but something had to happen to cause his mood change. As usual, it was different with Gertrud. She could be sitting there laughing, and suddenly her laughter could change into tears. Joel simply couldn't understand how laughter and tears could be inside a person at the same time.

He was never quite sure what to do when Gertrud's mood changed. It wasn't possible to talk to her, and he always wondered if he had said or done something wrong. But then it would pass just as quickly as it had happened.

He sat there, trying not to make it obvious that he was looking at her.

A sad, blue face.

Blue Gertrud.

Noseless Blue Gertrud.

He squirmed a little bit on his chair, and thought he ought to go home. Before going to sleep he could think up some good deed or other he could do the very next day.

But he didn't want to leave until Gertrud looked happy again.

Not tonight.

He tried to think of something that would make her happy.

Should he make her a cup of tea?

No, that wouldn't be enough.

Did he have a funny story he could tell her? Gertrud liked listening to stories about what he'd been doing. It didn't matter if he made it up, as long as it was exciting.

But he couldn't think of anything. His mind was a blank.

Then he noticed the dish full of blue paint.

He dipped his finger into it and started to write on his forehead. It wasn't easy, because the little mirror on the kitchen table he was using made everything look back to front. But with great difficulty he managed to write a couple of words on his forehead. Gertrud wasn't watching him. She was staring out of the window.

Eventually, he was ready. He saw that he had spelt one word wrong, but it wasn't possible to change it. It would have to do.

Gertrud was still staring out of the window. Joel could tell by the back of her neck that she was still sad.

The back of your neck can look sad, not just your face.

"Gertrud," he said tentatively, as if he was afraid she would become happy too quickly.

She didn't hear him.

"Gertrud," he said again, a bit louder this time.

She slowly turned round to look at him. It was a few seconds before she could read what he had written on his forehead.

GERTRUD HAPPY, it should have said.

But he had spelt it wrong.

What it actually said was: GERRUD HAPPY.

"I got it a bit wrong," he said. "But it's not easy to write backwards."

Gertrud was still looking serious. Joel hoped he hadn't made a mess of it.

He was just going to wipe the words off his forehead with the palm of his hand when that grim, blue face in front of him suddenly lit up and her white teeth shone through all the blue.

"I was only thinking," she said. "Now I'm happy again."

Joel couldn't help but smile broadly himself. The urge came from deep down inside him. Even though he was keeping his mouth tightly closed, he had started smiling.

Sometimes happiness just welled up inside you. Keeping your mouth tightly closed could do nothing to stop it.

"I'd better be going home now," he said.

Gertrud moistened a towel and wiped his forehead clean.

Joel closed his eyes and thought about Mummy Jenny's dress hanging at the back of Samuel's wardrobe.

Sometimes Gertrud had real mummy hands.

Then he walked back home. It wasn't quite so hard to cope with the Miracle any longer. He knew now what to do. He needed to think up some good deed or other that wouldn't take too long to do. Then he might be able to forget about that confounded bus. And about Eklund, who was good at shooting bears but wasn't careful enough when driving his bus.

Joel hurried up to the railway bridge. When he reached the other side, he paused and looked up at the stars.

But he didn't see a dog.

He wondered why Gertrud had become sad.

There again, it wasn't really surprising. Who wouldn't be sad if they didn't have a nose?

Or perhaps Gertrud was sad because she wasn't married and didn't have any children?

Joel put his hands in his pockets and started to trudge home.

He could think more about Gertrud and her blue face tomorrow morning. Right now he needed to think about a good deed he could do.

And also think about what to say if Samuel asked him what he and Eva-Lisa had been doing all evening...

— FOUR —

After school next day Joel paid a visit to Simon Windstorm. It was raining, and he was in a bad mood because
he hadn't been able to think of a good deed.

Why was it so difficult?

He'd started thinking about it that morning when
Samuel had shaken him by the shoulder and urged him to
hurry up and get dressed or he'd be late for school. There
hadn't been much time for thinking the night before.
When he got back home from Gertrud's, he found that
his father had spread out one of his old sea charts on the
kitchen table. He was using his chubby index finger to re-
trace the voyages he'd made years before.

Joel felt pleased when he entered the kitchen. When
his dad was studying sea charts, he was always in a good
mood. That meant he would be keen to tell stories about

his life as a seafarer. The pair of them would pore over the chart and relive the voyages.

Besides, Samuel never asked what Joel had been doing at Eva-Lisa's all evening. That was also good.

"The ship's due to sail in a couple of minutes," said Samuel as Joel came into the kitchen.

Joel hurried to take off his boots and jacket. Then he settled down on the wooden chair opposite Samuel, who was sitting on the kitchen bench.

"You were very nearly left behind," said Samuel, pretending to be stern.

The game had started. The serious game.

"Are you Joel Gustafson?" asked Samuel. "The new galley hand?"

"Yes," said Joel.

"Yes, Captain," said Samuel.

"Yes, Captain!" said Joel.

Then they set off. The mooring cables were cast off, the propeller started rotating, the sailors and deckhands scurried back and forth, the mates and bosuns barked out orders, and Captain Samuel Gustafson stood on the bridge, keeping an eye on everything.

Samuel had never been more than an able seaman, but when he went on a voyage with Joel he was always the captain.

"What's the name of the ship?" Joel asked.

Samuel peered at him over his glasses.

"Today we're sailing on the *Celestine*," he said. "The

finest ship of them all. But I've installed an engine in her so that we can go faster."

Joel glanced at the ship in its showcase beside the cooker.

He thought he could hear a creaking sound in the walls of the kitchen. As if the house were the ship that was slowly turning round in the dock and aiming her bow at the open sea.

Samuel placed his index finger on a spot on the sea chart.

"Scarborough Fair," he said. "Now we're leaving this dump."

"What's our cargo?" Joel wondered.

"Wild horses," said Samuel. "And iron ore. And some mysterious crates—only the captain knows what's inside them."

This is going to be a good voyage, Joel realized. Mysterious crates were the most exciting cargo you could possibly have. Only when you'd crossed over the ocean and reached the port you were heading for would you discover what was inside the crates.

"We'll pass to the north of the Orkneys," said Samuel, running his finger over the chart. "We'll have to keep a lookout for icebergs. If we run into a westerly gale we might be forced up as far as Iceland. But what the crew needs right now is a bowl of soup to warm them up."

Joel saw that Samuel had put a saucepan on the stove. Samuel produced two deep dishes and served up the soup.

He had made the soup from the remains of a leg of beef.

"Turtle soup," he said.

As they ate, the house heaved like a ship in a storm. The severe gale forced them as far north as the Icelandic coast: the high cliffs could just be made out through the raging and boiling waves. One member of the crew fell overboard, but they managed to fish him out of the water and haul him back on deck. Silent, majestic icebergs drifted past; the wild horses were neighing and kicking in the cages below deck. And all the time, Samuel was explaining what was happening. The raging of the storm, and the stillness afterwards. The flickering of sea fire during the nights. Meeting other ships, and the enormous whales spouting in the distance. Eventually, early one morning, they glimpsed the coast of Newfoundland, and were able to change course for Philadelphia. There they were met by a tug, and soon they were moored by the quay.

Samuel leaned back on the kitchen bench and straightened his back.

"A good voyage," he said. "But things could have turned out nasty for the deckhand who fell overboard."

"It was a miracle that we managed to get him back on board," said Joel.

"He was lucky," said Samuel. "Lucky, no more than that."

"What about those mysterious crates?" ventured Joel.

"Oh, I nearly forgot them," said Samuel, standing up and disappearing into his room.

Joel remained on his chair, tense with excitement.

Mysterious crates always resulted in Joel being given something by Samuel.

His dad returned to the kitchen.

"Those crates we were carrying contained old memories," he said.

He handed Joel a faded photograph.

It was dirty, and one corner was torn off. But Joel could see that it depicted a ship in port. Some of the crew were standing on a gangway, looking directly at the camera. One of them was in uniform; the rest were wearing normal working clothes.

One of the crewmen had moved his head just as the photograph was being taken. That's why his face was blurred.

"That's me," said Samuel, pointing to the blurred face. "Just as the photographer pressed the button, a fly flew up my nose. So there's a fly in this picture as well, even if you can't see it. I found this snap when I was searching for another one. That's the way it always is. You never find what you're looking for, but you find something else instead. I'd like you to have the photograph. The ship was called *Pilgrimme*, and came from Bristol."

"Thank you," said Joel, laying the photograph down carefully on the table.

This was a terrific present. He would be able to imagine all kinds of adventures on the basis of it.

Samuel sat down on the bench again and started darning a sock. Joel cleared the table, and suddenly felt very tired. He wouldn't have the strength to think about his good deed tonight. He could feel that he'd fall asleep the moment he snuggled down in bed.

He undressed, brushed his teeth and put on his nightshirt, which reached right down to his feet. Once he had settled down under the blankets, he shouted to his dad. Samuel came in with the sock in his hand, and sat down on the edge of the bed. The bed creaked under his weight.

"Do you think a lot about the accident?" he asked.

"No," said Joel. "I don't think about the bus at all."

But that wasn't quite true. It was there all the time, lurking behind all the other thoughts spinning round in his head. Sometimes it forced its way to the fore, and then it was like a beast of prey, threatening to pounce on him.

Joel tried not to think about it. But it was hard. Thoughts can't simply cease to be thought about, just like that. Especially nasty thoughts.

The worst thought of all was that a tree would fall on top of Samuel while he was working in the forest. Nothing could be worse than that. When Joel thought about it, he was sometimes so frightened that he almost started trembling. It was as if the tree had fallen already. And Joel could do nothing about it. He had learnt that you can't run away from the nasty thoughts that crop up in your mind.

Perhaps the bus would become one of those thoughts? One that never went away?

Samuel stroked him on the cheek and went back to the kitchen. Joel tried to think about the good deed he was going to do, but he was too tired. His thoughts jumped and scurried about, and he couldn't catch them.

It was like trying to catch a flock of sparrows jumping around a pool of water in the street. . . .

He didn't manage to think of a good deed. Even though he thought about it as hard as he could. On two occasions he was thinking so hard that he forgot to listen to what Miss Nederström was saying. But she didn't notice that he wasn't paying attention. Or perhaps she excused him because he had experienced a Miracle?

Everything was almost back to normal during the breaks. But only almost. His friends still looked at him in a slightly odd way. And Joel could feel that uncomfortable feeling of solemnity coming back.

After school he decided to pay a visit to Simon Windstorm. Perhaps Simon could suggest a good deed? He was also known as the Old Bricklayer, and lived in a broken-down house on the other side of the hospital. Unlike Gertrud, who was just odd, Simon really was a bit mad. He had been locked up in a secure hospital for many years because he was insane. Then he'd got better, and they let him out again. But a lot of people thought he was still mad, and a lot were frightened of him as well.

Not Joel, though.

Not since that time Simon had taken him to Four Winds Lake.

Joel turned off from the main road and followed a little path that wound its way through dense thickets of young fir trees. It was easy to get lost if you didn't know the way. Simon had made a hotchpotch of paths. It was a sort of labyrinth. If you didn't take the right one, you kept coming back to the main road again. Simon had done this on purpose so that he would be left in peace. He lived in an old smithy, and there were some locals who considered that he shouldn't be allowed to stay there. Sometimes ladies dressed all in black and wearing flat hats, as well as men also dressed all in black, would come to Simon's door and try to persuade him to move into an old people's home. They always came in groups because they were frightened of Simon. He could get very angry at times. Once, he had thrown a hen at the head of a lady wearing a flat hat. There was a clucking and cackling all over the house, and the outcome was that Simon was left in peace. But not for long. They soon started coming back again.

Joel didn't really know if the Flat Hats had any right to decide where Simon was allowed to live. But he had no doubt at all that they belonged to an enemy tribe.

You had to be wary of the Flat Hats.

54

As Joel made his way through the tall fir trees, keeping an eye on the paths so that he didn't take a wrong turning, it occurred to him that he would have to get himself a real friend. He couldn't carry on only mixing with grown-ups, especially as they weren't all there.

Not that he had any intention of deserting Gertrud and Simon.

It was just that he wanted to have a friend of his own age.

Suddenly he emerged from the dense fir trees. There in front of him was Simon's cottage, surrounded by a garden full of scrap iron and old machines. Also parked there was the ancient lorry in which Simon used to drive round town when he couldn't sleep at night.

Smoke was rising from the chimney, and a hen was pecking away on the porch.

Joel paused and took a look at Simon's pigsty. It was an old taxicab that he had converted into a sty. A little pink snout was sticking up where the windscreen had been once upon a time.

Joel knocked on the front door and went in. It always took him some time to get used to the smell inside Simon's house. It wasn't a pleasant smell. Joel had to breathe through his mouth so as not to feel sick.

He knew that Simon didn't get washed very often. And there were chickens running around in all the rooms. And a Norwegian elkhound gnawing away at its bones next to the stove.

Joel needed time to grow accustomed to the smell, but he usually managed it after a while.

Simon was sitting at the table reading a book when Joel arrived. That's what he was usually doing when Joel paid a visit. He would read with a pencil in his hand, and if he came across something he didn't like, he would rewrite it. Books were piled up all over the house. The hens used to lay eggs in among the books, and Joel sometimes helped Simon to find them.

Simon was wearing a thick fur coat. He wore it throughout the summer as well as the winter. He had a beard that sprouted out in all directions, and his hair stood on end.

When Joel came into the room Simon was busy altering the ending of a fat book. Joel knew that Simon didn't like being disturbed when he was writing. He crossed out chunks of text, and wrote a new version between the lines. Joel squatted down and stroked the elkhound while Simon was busy writing.

In the end, Simon threw down his pencil, turned to look at Joel and smiled.

"That's better," he said. "Now the book finishes as it ought to do."

"Are you allowed to make whatever changes you like in books?" Joel asked.

"Allowed and allowed," said Simon, scratching at his beard. "I don't bother about such minor matters."

Joel sat down on a stool by the table. Simon peered at

him. It occurred to Joel that Simon might not have heard about the accident. Simon didn't speak to many people, apart from Joel.

Simon could well be the only person in the whole of the little town who had heard nothing about the accident.

Joel told him what had happened. Simon frowned and listened. Joel moved his stool farther back from the table, as Simon smelled unusually awful today.

Maybe that could be a good deed? he thought.

Making sure that Simon took a proper bath.

But he rejected the thought. It could be a dangerous suggestion to make. Simon might start throwing hens around.

"I have to think up a good deed," said Joel. "If you've benefited from a Miracle, you have to do a good deed."

"I suppose you must," said Simon slowly. "What you've told me was awful!"

"I don't have any pain at all," said Joel. "I didn't even bite my tongue."

He suddenly noticed that Simon had tears in his eyes.

He had never seen that before.

Joel felt a lump in his throat.

"Awful," Simon muttered. "Awful, awful..."

"It was my own fault, really," said Joel. "I wasn't looking where I was going."

A hen fluttered up onto the table and deposited a large lump of bird poo in the middle of the page Simon had just rewritten. Joel couldn't help but giggle.

Simon wiped the tears from his eyes, and smiled as well.

"She's given it her seal of approval," he said.

"A good deed," said Joel, still giggling. "How do you think up a suitable good deed?"

"We must have a think," said Simon. "I think it's best if we put our glasses on."

Joel had forgotten all about that. Simon's Thinking Glasses.

They looked like ordinary glasses. The only difference was that the lenses were painted black. When you had them on, you couldn't see anything.

Simon stood up and looked round the room.

"I wonder where I've put them," he mumbled. He turned to look at Joel. "Where would I usually put my glasses?" he asked.

"On a shelf," suggested Joel, recalling where his dad usually put his glasses.

Simon nodded.

"A shelf," he said. "Where is there a shelf?"

Joel looked round. There were no shelves in the room.

"In the pantry," he suggested. "There are shelves in there."

"You're right," said Simon. "There are shelves in the pantry."

He vanished into the pantry. Joel could hear the clashing of dishes and the clattering of pans. The clinking of empty bottles and the rustling of paper bags. Then Joel heard a triumphant yell, and Simon reappeared with two pairs of glasses in his hand.

"Now we can think," he said. "And if that doesn't help, we can take the Seven-Windowed Wagon and drive out to the Four Winds Lake."

The Seven-Windowed Wagon was his ancient lorry. Simon claimed he'd named it after the king's finest coach.

They each put on the glasses. They were really old motor-bike goggles that fitted tightly on all sides. Everything was black, even though they hadn't closed their eyes.

"So, let's have a think," said Simon.

There wasn't a sound. The elkhound was snoozing under the table. A hen was pecking in a corner.

Joel tried to concentrate on thinking up a good deed.

In fact, he was finding it very hard not to start giggling again.

That was something he'd noticed recently. Whenever something serious was happening, he found it very hard not to start giggling. It was as if an invisible hand had started tickling the soles of his feet.

As soon as he thought about it, he started giggling.

I mustn't giggle, he told himself sternly.

That set him off giggling uncontrollably. The giggles just seemed to come bubbling up out of his mouth. As if they'd been flowing over a mass of giggles he had buried inside himself.

Simon will be angry, he thought.

It didn't help. He giggled away even so.

But Simon wasn't angry. Joel had the feeling that Simon was one of the very rare grown-ups who hadn't forgotten what it was like to be nearly twelve years old.

There weren't many who hadn't forgotten.

His dad, Samuel, had forgotten. But not Gertrud.

Miss Nederström had forgotten. But not Simon Windstorm.

"This is no good," said Simon. "We might as well take our glasses off."

Joel loosened the strap round the back of his neck that secured the goggles.

"We'll have to drive out to Four Winds Lake," said Simon.

In normal circumstances Joel would have been overjoyed to go with Simon to the mysterious lake hidden deep in the forest. He loved clambering into the passenger seat beside Simon.

But not today.

Today there was something holding him back.

It was as if Joel had become scared of big motor vehicles.

If he was a passenger in the big lorry, he could hardly be run over.

But perhaps they might run over somebody else?

No, he didn't want to go in the lorry today.

"I haven't time," he mumbled. "I have an appointment with my dad."

Simon nodded.

"I'm sorry I can't help you," he said. "But perhaps the bottom line is that you have to think of a good deed yourself."

Joel left.

It had stopped raining. Ragged clouds were scudding over the sky.

He took a wrong turning in the middle of the labyrinth, and ended up outside Simon's house again.

He felt angry, but set off once more. This time he made no mistake. The fir trees became less dense, and he emerged onto the main road.

Now he was tired of thinking about good deeds. He wished he'd been able to chase them off like you scare off a swarm of mosquitoes by flapping and waving your arms about.

If only that idiot Eklund hadn't been driving so carelessly, he thought. Then I wouldn't have had to experience that Miracle.

I have no time to mess about with good deeds, Joel thought. I have to find myself a good friend. And I want to be a better football player.

I haven't got the time.

He trudged homewards, kicking the gravel so hard that he hurt his toes.

Joel felt sorry for himself.

He didn't have a mother. Nor did he have any close friends. All he had was Simon Windstorm, who smelled something awful, and Gertrud, who didn't have a nose.

There were so many things he didn't have.

I'm like Gertrud, he thought. She doesn't have a nose, and I don't have a mum. . . .

He suddenly stopped dead, in the middle of the road.

Perhaps he'd just had a brilliant idea for a good deed.

He couldn't help Gertrud to find a new nose.

But it was obvious that she needed a man!

She was thirty years old, and unmarried. She didn't have any children.

Perhaps he could help her to find a husband!

That was it!

The good deed he would perform was to find a man for Gertrud. So that she didn't need to spend her evenings all alone. A man she could marry.

But where would he be able to find such a man?

It didn't take him long to find the answer to that.

The bar! Where Sara worked! Lots of men sat there all day long, drinking beer. He'd heard Sara complaining to Samuel that there were far too many unmarried men spending all their time in the bar when they weren't at work, drinking beer.

He was in a hurry now. He ran down the hill leading to the town center. There was the ironmonger's, and there was the shoe shop. And over there, on the corner, was the bar.

He'd been running so fast that he had to pause and get his breath back.

It suddenly dawned on him that he was standing in the

very spot where he'd set off over the street without look-ing. The very same place where the accident had been transformed into a Miracle.

That must mean I'm doing the right thing, he thought. Starting my good deed at the very same spot.

The bar door opened and Nyberg, the bouncer, came out and blew his nose into his fingers. Joel dodged quickly behind a parked car. He didn't want Nyberg to see him and start asking questions.

Nyberg cleared his throat and spat onto the pavement. Then he went back into the bar. Joel looked carefully in both directions before crossing over the street. At the back of the bar was a door that Sara had said he could use if he wanted to pay her a visit.

He hesitated for a moment.

Then he opened the door and went into the bar to find a man for Gertrud.

— FIVE —

Joel sometimes broke a cup or a dish when he was washing up after he and Samuel had eaten a meal.

But that was nothing compared with what Ludde broke.

Ludde was the owner of the bar. But he didn't mix with his customers; instead, he spent his time at the sink. He was small and fat, and his hands were always red and swollen because of the washing-up water.

There was a notice on the door leading into the kitchen at the rear of the bar saying that unauthorized persons were not permitted entry, but that didn't apply to Joel because Sara worked there. Joel didn't often use that door. It was always chaotic and noisy in the kitchen. Besides, he didn't like Sara and the other waitresses patting him on the head. Treating him almost as if he were Sara's own boy.

He didn't like being a Nearly Boy. And even if Sara was nice and Samuel was always in a good mood when he was together with her, Joel refused to pretend that Sara was his mother. His mum was called Jenny, and would always be called Jenny. Even if he never met her again for the rest of his life, he would never have another mum.

But he did sometimes go in through the forbidden door. And today he had an important errand. He had to find a man for Gertrud.

When he entered the kitchen, it was even more chaotic than usual. Ludde was bent over the sink, washing up like a madman. There was a rattling and clinking and clattering in the frothy water from glasses, cups, dishes and cutlery.

It was mostly glasses, as this was a bar, after all, and everybody was drinking beer. But the beer drinkers occasionally grew hungry and wanted food. Ludde did the cooking and the washing up at the same time. Only one dish was served in the bar, and it was always known as Ludde's Beef Stew. Sara had told Joel that Ludde had owned the bar for over twenty years, and he had served the same stew all that time. Joel used to study the big pot standing on the stove, and imagined it cooking for twenty years. Ludde had occasionally added some new bits of meat, and stirred the thick, brown gravy; but essentially it was the same dish that had been standing on the stove for twenty years. Once, when Joel was hungry, Sara had served him up a plate of Ludde's Beef Stew. Joel had eaten it, and thought how he had eaten something that had been simmering on that stove since before he was born.

Now, when Joel entered the kitchen, Ludde was bent over the sink as usual.

"Joel!" he shouted. "You can't imagine how pleased we all were to hear that you hadn't been injured."

"No doubt it was a Miracle," said Joel evasively.

Just then Sara came in through the swing doors carrying a tray. It was full of empty bottles and glasses, overflowing ash trays and sticky plates. Joel wondered if he would have been able to lift the tray.

Sara was strong. Joel had once watched her heave a sack of coal onto her shoulder. His dad, Samuel, was strong, but Joel wondered if Sara was even stronger.

All the waitresses working in the bar were strong, and they all looked similar. Big and fat and sweaty. And they were all dressed the same: black skirts and white blouses. Once Joel had been in the kitchen and they had come in through the swing doors one after another, and it seemed to him that they looked like animals. Black-and-white waitress-elephants marching in from the beery jungle...

Sara put the tray down with a bang, and immediately, Ludde started filling his sink with more plates and glasses.

A dish and a glass fell off the tray and smashed as they hit the floor.

Joel hardly dared look in case he burst out laughing. There were always piles of broken china and glass round Ludde's feet. To avoid cutting his feet, he wore black overshoes. He didn't have shoes inside the overshoes, though, but slippers. As Joel wasn't really sure if Ludde minded people laughing at him, he avoided looking at the floor. Instead, he screwed up his eyes and peered sideways at the scene. He wouldn't need to laugh if he did that.

Sara had told Joel that all the money Ludde earned by selling beer and beef stew was spent on buying new crockery and glasses. Once Sara and the other waitresses had been paid, and Nyberg the bouncer as well, and all the beer and the stew bills had been settled, Ludde only had enough money left over to buy new crockery and glasses.

And it went on like that, year after year. And all the time the pot of stew clucked and spluttered on the stove.

"Hello, Joel," said Sara with a smile, wiping the sweat from her brow.

Please don't hug me, Joel thought. I don't want to be hugged.

"Have you come to visit me?" said Sara, pulling him closer and giving him a hug. Joel tried to resist, but it was impossible. Sara was as strong as a weight lifter.

She could have toured the fairgrounds in a sideshow as Sara the Strong.

"Are you hungry?" she asked. "Would you like something to eat?"

"No thank you," said Joel. "I only called in to say hello."

He didn't really know how to go about finding a man for Gertrud, nor did he know if Sara would be able to help him. That's why he answered as he did.

As he ran down the hill from Simon Windstorm's house, he'd tried to gather his thoughts on what he knew about how grown-ups came to meet one another. He found it difficult to understand anything to do with love. To be honest, he had a pretty good idea of what was involved. At school, behind the bicycle sheds, Otto had once condescended to explain to Joel and some other boys how children were made. Joel had listened carefully, so as not to miss a single word. At first he thought that Otto must be out of his mind. Could that *really* be what happened? Surely not? How was it *really* done?

Joel had been sensible enough not to ask any questions, but for a long time he doubted if Otto had been telling the truth. Later, when he'd heard the same story from others, he had realized that it must presumably be right, strange though it might seem. Strange and complicated. He'd spent a lot of time wondering how there could possibly be so many children around when the whole business seemed to be so complicated.

So Joel knew quite a lot. And he knew how you went about kissing, even if he hadn't yet tried it on a girl, only on his own reflection in the mirror.

But the big question was: how do grown-ups get to meet one another?

He knew some of the answer. You could go to the dance at the Community Center on Saturday night, when Kringström's orchestra was playing. That's where people met. And he'd read in books about other ways in which people could meet. In fairy tales princes climbed up long ropes to meet princesses who were locked in high towers.

But in the little town he lived in the only towers were the church steeple and the red tower at the fire station where the firemen used to hang up their hose pipes to dry. Joel found it hard to imagine Gertrud sitting at the top of the Fire Brigade tower without a nose.

But there were other ways in which grown-ups could meet. In most of the books he read there were always some chapters describing how people met and eventually got married. But there was never anything about what Otto had described behind the bicycle sheds. Joel assumed that was because it was so boring to write about it.

You could meet in the wreckage of a train that had fallen into a ravine. You could rescue a girl who had fallen into freezing water when the ice broke, and later marry her. You could wear a black mask and kidnap a girl.

There were lots of ways. But by the time Joel had come to the bottom of the hill and paused to regain his breath before entering the back door of the bar, he had decided that the best place for Gertrud to meet the man he hadn't yet found for her was probably the Community Center.

Joel sat down on a chair in the corner where he was least in the way. Sara had vanished through the swing doors again, carrying a tray full of beer bottles. He tried to think up a good way of getting Sara to help him, without her realizing it. If he could get her to tell him about the men sitting out there in the bar, which ones were unmarried and which ones were nice, he'd be able to choose the one he thought would be most suitable for Gertrud.

But what characteristics would be most suitable for Gertrud?

What kind of man would she most like to have?

It wasn't easy to think in the kitchen, with Ludde creating havoc at the sink all the time. And Sara and the other waitresses running in and out, emptying trays and loading them up again with new bottles and glasses.

"I'll soon be coming for a sit-down," said Sara, before disappearing with her tray.

The other two waitresses, Karin and Hilda, said the same thing.

"We'll soon be coming for a sit-down and a rest."

Joel didn't say anything. He was regretting not having waited a bit longer before coming to the bar. He ought to

70

have thought through what kind of man Gertrud would want first. Then he should have worked out how Sara could be tricked into helping him.

This was typical of Joel—he often forgot to think before starting to do something.

And this was the result. Just then Ludde dropped another glass that shattered on the checked tile floor.

"Now!" exclaimed Sara, throwing down her tray and slumping onto a chair. "Time for a rest!"

She poured herself a cup of coffee, put a lump of sugar in her mouth and started slurping. Then she looked up at Joel, and smiled.

"I'm so pleased," she said. "So pleased that nothing happened to you. You wouldn't believe how much the blokes out there are talking about the accident. You've given them something to talk about. Everybody knows who Joel Gustafson is now."

Joel couldn't make up his mind if that was a good thing or a bad thing.

Perhaps in future people would turn round in the street to look at him and think: there goes that Joel Gustafson, who was run over by the Ljusdal bus without suffering a single scratch.

Maybe they would even give him a nickname. Like Mr. Under the horse dealer, who was only ever referred to as Neighing Ned.

Or Hugo, who was an electrician and the best player on the local ice hockey team.

How many people knew that his name was Hugo, when everybody called him Snotty?

The world is full of nicknames, Joel thought. Snotty and Fleabag Frankie and Paintpot Percy, who was a painter and decorator. There was a chimney sweep known to everybody as Jim even though his real name was Anders. Not to mention the baker everybody called Bluebottle, because he had a front tooth missing and made a buzzing sound when he talked. Or the stone-mason known as Buggery, because that was more or less all he ever said. Or the vicar whose name was Nikodemus but was called Knickers by those who knew him. But most people just said Vicar. Then there was a skier known as Skater Sammy, and a drayman nicknamed Pop. But oddest of all was surely the carpenter called Johanson who was known to everybody as the Welder.

What would Joel's nickname be?

Joel *Ljusdal* Gustafson?

Lucky Joel?

Miracle Gustafson?

Joel frowned, and pulled a face at the very thought.

That was the worst thing about nicknames—it was always somebody else who invented them.

You ought to be able to choose your own nickname.

"What are you pulling a face at?" asked Sara, with a laugh.

"Nothing," said Joel.

"It was nice of you to come and visit me."

"I wanted to ask you something," said Joel, without knowing what he wanted to ask her about.

Sara nodded, and looked at him.

Just then the swing doors were flung open and Karin came storming into the kitchen. She was red in the face with anger.

"I can't make head nor tail of that lot," she said. "Now two of them have started thumping each other."

Ludde broke off his washing up and turned to look at her.

"What's Nyberg doing about it?" he asked. "Why doesn't he throw them out?"

"He tried," said Karin. "But now he's on the floor with the other two on top of him."

Before they knew where they were, everybody was rushing towards the swing doors. Joel had stood up and followed Sara, but when she got as far as the doors she turned round and said sternly:

"You stay here."

Joel was angry at not being allowed to go with them. But at the same time, he had to admit that he was a bit scared.

He peered cautiously through the crack in the doors.

Tables and chairs were overturned all over the floor. Nyberg the bouncer was just crawling out from underneath a mass of arms and legs. He was rubbing his nose and looking furious. Sara had taken hold of one of the drunks, and was shaking him as if he were a little boy.

Ludde was waving his red hands about and shouting something Joel couldn't make out.

He wasn't at all sure who had been fighting.

On the other hand, he noticed two men sitting calmly at a table, apparently completely unconcerned by what had been going on. They were drinking pilsner, both leaning forward with heads close together, and talking away. One of them was fair-haired. It struck Joel that he looked very like the blond boy depicted on tubes of one of Sweden's favorite delicacies, Kalle's Caviar. (It wasn't the expensive, "real" caviar, but what you might call the poor man's caviar—fish roe, delicious with your breakfast toast.) The man was the spitting image of Kalle, despite the fact that he was probably three times as old. His friend had dark hair, combed in Elvis Presley style.

They are the ones, Joel thought.

One of them could become Gertrud's husband!

He would have liked to continue spying on them through the crack in the doors, but Ludde and Sara were striding back towards the kitchen again. Bouncer Nyberg had thrown out the two troublemakers through the big front door. Karin and Hilda were busy clearing up after the fight.

Joel scurried back to his chair.

Ludde returned to the sink, and started by dropping a plate that smashed on the floor. Sara flopped down on her chair, produced a handkerchief from her cleavage and mopped her face.

"What happened?" asked Joel, trying to give the impression that he'd been sitting on his chair all the time.

Sara leaned forward and whispered:

"I saw you peeping out through the doors."

Joel blushed. He felt as if he'd turned red all the way from his stomach up to his forehead.

His first reaction was to deny that he'd been looking.

But he changed his mind immediately. He'd only have blushed even more.

"It wasn't all that serious," said Sara. "When they've cooled down they'll be as meek as lambs again."

"Why did they start fighting?" Joel asked. He didn't like the fact that Sara had caught him out.

"I've no idea," said Sara with a shrug. "Have you?"

The latter question was directed at Karin, who had just come in through the swing doors with a shovel in her hand.

"Do I have any idea about what?" asked Karin.

"Why they were fighting?"

Karin emptied her shovel into a bin standing between the stove and the sink, where Ludde was splashing about with his plates and glasses.

"It was something to do with a girl," said Karin. "Blokes only fight if there's a girl involved, don't they?"

Joel listened with his eyes open wide.

"I think they're both sweet on the same girl," said Karin. "That Anneli who works in the shoe shop."

"Is she anything to fight over?" asked Hilda, who had joined them in the kitchen.

She turned to look at Joel.

"Or what do you think, Joel?" she asked. "Surely a shop assistant in a shoe shop isn't worth fighting over?"

All the waitresses laughed, and Ludde dropped another glass on the floor.

Joel could feel himself blushing again. He thought he would have to say something that showed he'd understood what they were getting at.

"I shall never fight over anybody who sells shoes," he said. "Never."

They all laughed again, and Hilda came up to pat his head. Joel tried to shrink away, but she left her hand there and ruffled his hair.

"He's as nice as Rolf and David," she said. "The girls who get them can consider themselves lucky."

Then she sat down at the table alongside Sara and Karin. Joel listened to what they said. He had realized that it was sometimes important to hear what grown-ups were saying. They sometimes said things you could learn something from. Not very often. But sometimes. Such as now.

It dawned on Joel that they were talking about the two young men sitting at a table by themselves and paying no attention at all to the violent fight taking place.

"If only I were a bit younger," sighed Hilda, as she massaged her tired feet.

"I wish they'd been my sons," said Karin.

Sara said nothing. But she nodded in agreement. All the time Ludde was clattering away at the sink.

Joel stood up and tried to sneak out of the door without being seen.

He didn't see the bucket standing next to his chair, and stumbled over it. He fell headlong and ended up in the middle of the three waitresses.

"A boy's paying us a flying visit," said Hilda, with a laugh.

Joel could feel that he was blushing again.

He had blushed more today than he'd ever done before.

Karin stood up, took her tray and vanished through the swing doors again.

Hilda went to the storeroom and began carrying in new crates of beer.

"What was it you were going to ask me about?" Sara wondered.

"Does one of them look like the caviar tube?" asked Joel.

Sara looked at him in astonishment.

"What do you mean? The caviar tube? Who's supposed to look like a caviar tube?"

"David or Rolf? Like the boy on the caviar tube?"

Then the penny dropped. She burst out laughing and slapped her knee.

"You must be referring to David," she said. "You're right, he does look like the lad with the mop of blond hair on the caviar tube."

"I just wondered," said Joel. "I must be off. Bye!"

And he hurried out of the door before Sara had time to ask him anything else.

It was already starting to get dark outside. Joel raised the collar of his jacket and ran round the corner to check the time on the church clock.

Five o'clock already!

He had better hurry up and put the potatoes on. Samuel was usually home by six at the latest. The potatoes had to be ready by then.

David and Rolf would have to wait. He was in a hurry. . . .

It was evening. Joel could hear Samuel in the room next door listening to the radio. Joel was sitting like a tailor on his bed, writing up the logbook he had taken from the *Celestine*'s showcase.

He wasn't actually writing, in fact. He'd already finished.

"There was trouble at the bar today. . . . "

That was as far as he'd got. He'd had the feeling that it was silly, keeping a logbook. He started reading it instead. He had glued the edges of some pages and drawn a red stamp on them, saying that what was written there had to be kept secret for a year. But he hadn't paid any attention to that. Declaring part of your own diary secret was child-ish and not something anybody who would soon be twelve could indulge in.

TSFTDTHFAS, it said on the cover.

The Search for the Dog That Headed for a Star.

His Secret Society.

He read bits here and there in the book and thought that all he had written about seemed to have happened a very long time ago. In fact, it was only just over six months ago. Barely even that.

He didn't like the idea of time passing so quickly. Of everything changing so quickly. Not least himself. He would really prefer everything to stay the same. You ought to be able to pick out a day when everything had gone well and say: It's always going to be like this!

But that wasn't possible! Why wasn't it possible?

Joel sighed and dropped the diary on the bed in front of him.

Perhaps that was the way you became a grown-up? By realizing that there was no such thing as a day that could never be changed?

Perhaps that's why so many grown-ups looked so tired and miserable? Because they knew that's the way things are?

He jumped impatiently off the bed and lay stretched out on the floor, looking at the maps he had cut up. He tried to think a bit more about the geography game. But that wasn't much fun either. Then he lay on his back and stared up at the ceiling. He traced the outlines of the damp patches with his eyes.

He suddenly felt as if he were lying underneath the bus again.

Just think if he'd died!

He wouldn't have been able to smell the awful stench in Simon Windstorm's house anymore. Or to sit with his dad, Samuel, at the kitchen table and sail the seven seas.

He would never have fallen asleep again, never woken up.

He didn't like those thoughts. They were scurrying around in his head like ants. He sat up and thought he ought to go to bed now.

What he would have liked to do most of all would have been to give up all thoughts of doing a good deed. Gertrud could find herself a man without his help, if she wanted one. She could brick herself into the church tower and wait for somebody to climb up to her. . . .

Curse that Miracle, he thought.

In any case, surely it should be Eklund who ought to do a good deed?

He was the one who caused it all, and was lucky enough not to have killed a human being with his bus.

But deep down, Joel knew that he was the one who would have to do a good deed. So he might as well get it over with as soon as possible.

He clambered back onto his bed and started writing in his logbook:

"Today I, Joel Gustafson, who don't yet have a nickname, have decided that Gertrud must have a man. Finding one for her will be my good deed in return for the Miracle. I have chosen David or Rolf to become her husband. All I have to do now is to establish which one of them is most suitable."

He read through what he had written. That would do. It was more than enough.

"Shouldn't you be going to bed now, Joel?" shouted Samuel from his room. Joel could hear that he had adjusted the radio so that there was no program, only static. His dad used to do that when he wanted to listen to the sea.

"In a minute," Joel shouted in reply. "I've started."

Although the town they lived in was very small, he had never seen David and Rolf before. He didn't know their surnames, where they lived or what their work was.

What would he do if they lived a hundred miles away?

I'll have to start tomorrow, he thought. I'll ask Otto. He knows everybody's name.

He went to the kitchen and replaced the logbook in the *Celestine's* showcase. Then he got undressed, brushed his teeth and settled down in bed.

At first it was so cold that he had to tense every muscle in his body. But it gradually grew warmer under the covers.

"I'm in bed now," he shouted to Samuel.

His dad came shuffling into Joel's room in his slippers.

"Dad," said Joel, "have you ever had a nickname?"

Samuel looked at him in surprise.

"Why do you ask that?"

"I just wondered."

Samuel shook his head.

"When I was a sailor I suppose there were a few ship-mates who called me Sam," he said. "But you can hardly call that a nickname."

"Has Mum got a nickname?" Joel asked.

He was surprised by his own question. It just came tumbling out of its own accord.

Samuel looked serious.

"No," he said. "She was called Jenny. Nothing else."

Joel sat bolt upright.

"That's wrong," he said.

"What's wrong?" asked Samuel in surprise.

"It's not 'she was called Jenny,'" he said. "She *is* called Jenny."

Samuel nodded slowly.

"Yes," he said. "She is called Jenny. You're right. Go to sleep now."

Samuel stroked him lightly over the cheek, and went back to his own room, then into the kitchen. He left the kitchen door ajar. A narrow strip of light shone onto Joel's bed.

Joel always used to lie and contemplate that strip of light before going to sleep.

He could hear Samuel pouring warm water into the washbasin.

It was a procedure that never changed. It was the same night after night, for as long as Joel could remember.

He could feel his eyelids growing heavy.

The last thought he had before falling asleep was that he wasn't looking forward to asking Otto about David's and Rolf's surnames. Or where they lived.

You should always steer well clear of Otto. He teased and bullied everybody, and did stupid things.

But who else could he ask?

He rolled over to face the wall, and curled up under the covers.

The next day he would start his hunt for the Caviar Man and his friend.

— SIX —

It turned out just as Joel had foreseen.

Needless to say, Otto caused endless problems.

It was the second break when Joel plucked up enough courage to approach Otto on the playground. Otto was busy trying to exchange a rusty sheath knife for a pair of old motorbike gloves. Joel hung back until the deal had been settled. He watched Otto stuff the gloves into his jacket pocket with a self-satisfied grin, then went up to him.

"I'd like a word with you," Joel said.

Otto gave him a withering look.

"You mean you can come out with words?" he said scornfully. "I thought small fry like you could only whimper."

Joel was tempted to sock him one, but manfully refrained. That was exactly what Otto wanted: for boys smaller than himself to start a fight. Then he could beat them up and later defend himself by saying that he wasn't the one who'd started it.

"I'd like to ask you something," said Joel. "If you can give me an answer, I'll give you two picture cards."

Joel knew that Otto collected picture cards of footballers. He'd made up his mind to sacrifice the pictures he'd found inside the packs of pastilles he'd been given by Sara.

Otto was still suspicious.

"Honest," said Joel. "I'm not having you on."

"If you are, you'll get a good thumping," said Otto, setting off for the back of the school, where the bicycle sheds were.

The bicycle sheds were the school's law courts. Only the senior boys were allowed to go there. Girls were forbidden. And no junior boys, unless they were accompanied by a senior.

"Show me the pictures," said Otto, turning to face Joel.

Joel knew that the situation was now crucial. If he wasn't careful, Otto would snatch the picture cards and run off without having answered any questions. That's why he took a step backwards, and produced just one of the pictures.

"That's only one," said Otto.

"I have another one," said Joel. "But I want an answer to my questions first."

"What questions?"

Joel shook his head and continued round the corner. He leaned against the wall of the bicycle shed and forced himself to look Otto in the eye.

"There are two young men called Rolf and David," Joel said. "They spend a lot of time in the bar. One of them looks like the boy on the Kalle's Caviar tube. What are their surnames? Where do they live? Where do they work?"

"That's three questions," said Otto with a grin. "I want three picture cards."

Joel couldn't think of a good answer.

"If you ask three questions, you can have one answer free," he said somewhat hesitantly.

Otto was still grinning.

"Who says so?"

"That's the way it is in the big wide world," said Joel. "But maybe you don't know how it is in the big wide world?"

That was a dangerous answer. Otto could turn nasty and start fighting. Joel took his hands out of his pockets and prepared to defend himself.

But Otto just kept on grinning.

"Of course I know how it is in the big wide world," he said. "Don't think you can teach me anything."

I fooled him, Joel thought triumphantly. Not many people manage to do that!

"Why do you want to know about them?" said Otto.

"That's none of your business."

"Then I shan't tell you."

"Then you won't get any picture cards."

Otto shrugged.

"Rolf's name is Person," he said. "He lives near the Highways Department workshops, with his mum. He does any work that comes along."

"What do you mean, any work that comes along?"

"I mean what I say! Any work that comes along!"

Joel realized that Otto didn't know.

"What about the other one?" he asked.

"I think his name's Lundberg," said Otto. "He works for the council, catching rats."

Joel was very doubtful. He'd never heard of anybody being paid for catching rats.

"Come on, nobody works as a rat catcher!"

"Of course they do! Are you suggesting that I'm telling lies?"

Otto took a step forward and looked threatening.

"Of course I don't think you're lying," said Joel, but he couldn't stop his voice from shaking.

"He keeps the sewers clean. He lives in a shed in Lasse the Cabbie's backyard. If you know where that is."

"Of course I know where Lasse the Cabbie lives!"

Otto held out his giant-size hand.

"The picture cards," he said.

Joel took them out of his jacket pocket and put them in Otto's hand. Otto put them in his inside pocket. Then he stepped forward and grabbed hold of the lapels of Joel's jacket.

"Now you're going to get a good thumping," he said.

At that very moment the bell rang. Break was over.

Otto let go of Joel's jacket.

"Another time," he said. "I'll give you a good thumping some other time. Because you ask too many questions."

The rest of the day Joel had no time to think about what Otto had told him. Miss Nederström was in a bad mood, and Joel was no longer sure that his Miracle would protect him from her wrath.

After school Joel went with some of his classmates to take a look at a new car that was on display in Krage's Car Showrooms. It was a shiny black Pontiac, and they stood for ages gaping through the window, wondering who would be able to afford a car like that.

It was quite late by the time Joel got home and started peeling the potatoes.

Only then did he remember that today was the day he ought to have collected his bicycle, which had been in for repairs.

How on earth could he have forgotten his bike?

He looked at the kitchen clock. If he ran he still had time to get to the cycle shop before it closed. But then he remembered that he'd forgotten to ask Samuel for some money that morning. And he knew that the owner of the cycle shop never allowed credit.

The bike would have to wait.

Joel sat down on the kitchen bench and thought about what Otto had said. But which one should he start with?

Rolf or David? Before he could make up his mind which of them was best for Gertrud, he would have to spy on them.

He jumped down from the kitchen bench, went into the hall and started to search through Samuel's pockets. He found a five-öre piece in one of them. He took it into the kitchen and decided that Rolf was heads, and David was tails. Then he spun the coin round on the kitchen table.

Heads. He would start with Rolf tomorrow.

"Are you going out again? You go running off every night nowadays!" said Samuel after dinner, when Joel started pulling on his Wellingtons.

"I won't be long," said Joel.

"Where are you going?"

Joel thought quickly.

"To Eva-Lisa's," he said. It was the best answer he could come up with.

Samuel lowered his newspaper and peered at Joel over his reading glasses.

"You're spending a lot of time round at her place. Have you started getting interested in girls already?"

Joel blushed.

He turned his back on Samuel as he buttoned up his jacket.

"Yes," he said. "I'm probably going to marry her in a few years' time."

Then he left.

He could see from the corner of his eye how Samuel gaped in astonishment and his chin almost hit his neck.

Serves him right for asking an unnecessary question, Joel thought cheerfully.

It was cold outside. The sky was clear and the stars twinkling. Joel didn't really know how he was going to go about spying on Rolf, to find out if he was a suitable man for Gertrud.

Should he ring the doorbell, introduce himself and explain how things were? That he was looking for a suitable husband for Gertrud? That doing so was to be his good deed in return for shaking off the Miracle that he had experienced?

No, he couldn't do that, of course.

Rolf would think that he had a screw loose.

Joel crept though the hole in the pharmacy fence that he had once made himself, using an old pair of secateurs. Then he followed the row of currant bushes facing the courtyard in front of the furniture shop. There was a little shed there, and if he climbed onto its roof he would be able to see the house behind the Highways Department workshops where Rolf lived with his mother. He crept cautiously along the row of currant bushes. The furniture dealer had quite a temper, and Joel had learnt to avoid annoying him. He listened carefully in the darkness. Then he heaved himself up onto the roof. He had worked out that Rolf must live on the ground floor, and there was a retired schoolmistress in the flat upstairs. Those were the only two flats in the building.

He peered at the ground floor windows. It was getting exciting now.

He slowly raised his head and saw the fires glowing in the distance. General Custer in person had given him this mission. He couldn't return until he had reconnoitered all aspects of the Indian camp. He was well aware that if he was captured, there would be no going back. He would die.

He could see right in through the windows. The curtains were not drawn. A woman was sitting in a chair, knitting. A kitten was playing with the ball of wool at her feet. Joel was close enough to see that she was making a pair of gloves. A pair of red gloves.

But where was Rolf? Joel shifted his gaze to the next window.

There he was!

He was in the kitchen, doing the washing up. Wearing an apron.

Joel pulled a face.

A man standing at the sink and doing the washing up was not what he'd had in mind for Gertrud.

The enemy is weak, he thought. Just now the Indian camp contains nothing but old ladies. He could go back to the general and advise him to attack immediately, before the men had returned from their hunting expedition on the distant prairie.

He stayed on the roof for a while longer. But nothing happened. The woman on the chair knitted. The kitten played. And Rolf washed up. When he'd finished, he served his mother a cup of coffee. Then he lay down on the sofa to read the newspaper. The same paper that Samuel used to read. Nothing exciting. Not a magazine about motorcars, or sport. Just the local newspaper that was full of pictures of people waving or holding hands.

Joel started to feel cold, so he jumped down from the shed roof.

Rolf was not the man. Joel was tempted to send Rolf a secret message, telling him he was not up to scratch. A message Joel would sign with his own blood.

He made his way slowly back to the street, and trudged back home. He would spy on David after school on Monday.

What would he do if David, the Caviar Man, turned out to be equally boring?

What would he need to do then, in order to find a man for Gertrud?

He had no idea.

On Monday morning, the ground was white with frost.

Joel glared crossly out of the window. Perhaps it wasn't real snow, nor was it real winter yet; but it was too early even so.

Earlier in the year Joel had really looked forward to the first snow. There was something special about the morning when he raised the blind and saw the first snow of the winter. But not when it was this early. Not when it was still only September.

Samuel also heaved a sigh.

"Ah well," he said. "Before long we'll have to start plodding through the snow."

Joel wondered if he ought to say what he was thinking—that if Samuel hadn't been stupid enough to stop being a sailor, he could have been standing on a swaying deck under a Caribbean sky. Not just Samuel, but Joel as well.

But he didn't say it. Not when he needed to ask for money to pay for the bicycle repairs.

Samuel produced his purse and handed him a five-kronor note.

"I don't think that'll be enough," said Joel. "It'll cost ten at least."

Samuel sighed and gave him a tenner instead.

Samuel always sighed when Joel asked for money. Joel had resolved never to sigh when any children he might eventually have asked him for money.

Samuel set off downstairs, and Joel sat back with his mug of hot chocolate.

He thought about Rolf, doing the washing-up and wearing an apron.

Let's hope the Caviar Man wasn't as wet.

He looked at the clock, and jumped to his feet. He'd

been wasting too much time again. Now he'd have to run as fast as he could in order to avoid being late for school.

He cursed as he put on his jacket.

Why could he never learn?

Even though he ran for all he was worth, he was late. The classroom door was shut, and he could hear the harmonium playing the morning hymn. He hung up his jacket and curled up on the window ledge of one of the corridor windows. He'd have to wait. There was no way he could enter the classroom during morning prayers. That was one way of ensuring that Miss Nederström would pull his hair.

Joel gazed out over the school yard, glittering white with frost.

Could he think up a good excuse for being late?

Should he blame it on the Miracle? Claim that it was so difficult to cope with it that his legs didn't have the strength to move quickly?

He shook his head at his own thought. Miss Nederström wouldn't be fooled by that. If she was really annoyed she might make him march round and round the classroom so that everybody could see his tired legs. And Otto would sit there sniggering....

The harmonium stopped playing. Joel jumped down from the window ledge. He raised his hand to knock on the door.

Inside there were beasts of prey waiting to pounce on him.

He lowered his hand.

I'm ill, he thought. The good deed I have to carry out is making me ill.

That was it. He wouldn't go to school today.

He recovered his jacket and sneaked out through the door.

To make sure nobody would see him, he crouched down below window level until he had turned the corner.

When he emerged into the street, he felt well and truly relieved. He had made a good decision. He could afford to be off school for one day. Stomachache could strike very quickly. He could have got it after Samuel had gone to work. He'd been stricken by the gripes while he was finishing his breakfast. Nothing serious. But bad enough for him not to go to school.

Now he had a whole day to himself. The first thing he would do was to collect his bike. Then he could do whatever he liked until two o'clock. School finished then, and there was a risk that he might bump into Miss Nederström after two. But until then, he could do whatever he wanted.

He felt the ten-kronor note he had in his pocket.

He suddenly had an idea. He wasn't sure that it would work, but it could be worth trying.

Old Man Johanson was opening his newsagent's. Joel watched him removing the shutters from the display windows. There was a parcel of newspapers on the pavement.

Old Man Johanson spotted Joel and pointed to the parcel.

"The placards," he said. "Pin 'em up."

Joel squatted down and started untying the knot in the string round the newspapers. It was a granny knot and almost impossible to unravel. He noticed a rusty nail almost hidden by some stones. He stuck the nail into the knot and twisted and prodded until it came loose and he could remove the yellow placards. As he was pinning them onto the display boards he read the headlines. It said in big black letters that an agreement had been reached.

Who had agreed, about what?

You had to read the newspaper in order to find out.

It could have said instead: *"Joel Gustafson's Miracle."*

"Joel Gustafson's Struggle to Do His Good Deed."

"Rolf Not Up to It, Gustafson Decides."

"Will the Caviar Man Come Up to Scratch?"

"Who Will Be Gertrud's Man? Watch This Space!"

Joel lifted up the parcel and put it on the counter. Old Man Johanson gave him a bottle of Coke for his efforts.

"Can you change this for me?" he asked, holding out the ten-kronor note. "I need a five-kronor note, and five one-krona coins."

Old Man Johanson opened the cash register and counted out the money.

"Why aren't you at school today?" he asked.

"Our teacher's ill," said Joel.

That was a good answer. It could easily be true, and it was difficult to check.

But no doubt Old Man Johanson had forgotten all about it already. He was busy sorting out the newspapers.

Joel hurried off to the cycle shop.

It would be exciting to see if his idea worked.

The bell rang as Joel opened the door. The owner came out from the workshop.

"I've come to collect my bike," said Joel. "The red one with the broken chain."

The man disappeared into the workshop, then came back with Joel's bike.

There was a sheet of paper fastened to the saddle.

"That'll be ten kronor, please," he said.

"But I've only got eight kronor," said Joel, trying to sound devastated. His voice was little more than a squeak.

"It costs ten kronor," said the man. "That's what it says here, on the note. I wrote it myself."

Joel tried to look as if he were about to burst out crying.

It worked.

"All right, give me eight kronor. But it should be ten. I wrote it myself on this note."

Joel gave him eight kronor, and wheeled his bike out of the shop.

Two kronor wasn't bad.

The day had started well. He'd pulled off a good deal, and he didn't have a bad conscience about not going to school.

He mounted his bike, and tried a few test skids on the gravel road leading down to the river. The chain felt good. Now he could try to track down the Caviar Man. He pulled up next to a round iron lid in the middle of the street. Maybe the Caviar Man was down there in the Underworld, with all his rats? Joel would lift up the manhole cover and shout down to him.

Everything suddenly became very exciting.

Joel had never imagined that there was an Underworld even in this dump. Underground tunnels and great big pipes and enormous rats hissing through their whiskers.

He would be able to clamber down into a hole and disappear. All the buildings and streets and people would be up above him. Perhaps there would even be a tunnel running underneath his school? Under Miss Nederström's feet?

He looked round. Would he dare to open the lid and climb down?

There were too many people around who could see him. You only visited the Underworld when there was nobody to see what you were doing.

Joel got back onto his bike and cycled to the red-painted Municipal Offices on the other side of the vicarage, on a slope down to the river. He parked his bike in a stand labeled VISITORS TO THE MUNICIPAL OFFICES. He opened the front door and went in.

He found himself in a large entrance hall with a stone floor. A broad staircase led to the first floor. The walls were lined with pictures of stern gentlemen, all of them frowning at him. He listened. Not a sound. Behind a glass panel was a little room, and he could see a telephone receiver hanging down, and swinging slowly from side to side. Joel went to investigate and realized that it was a switchboard.

The receiver was still swinging back and forth.

Joel had the feeling that he was on a ghost ship. Somebody had let go of the handset and jumped overboard.

He listened again. Still not a sound. When he walked over the stone floor all he could hear was a faint squeaking noise from his Wellingtons. He came to a corridor. A door was standing ajar—it had a sign saying HEAD CLERK. Joel peeped inside, but the office was empty. He continued down the corridor. The next door was closed. And the next. Then came a door that was wide open. A sign said MUNICIPAL ENGINEER. Joel stepped inside. The walls were covered by bookshelves and map racks. There was a large map opened out on the desk, looking like a sea chart. Joel took a closer look. It was the plan of a house.

Joel turned round to leave the room, but found there was a man standing in the doorway.

Joel gave a start.

The man was wearing dark blue overalls. Joel noticed that he was in his bare feet.

"Is the engineer not here?" asked the man.

"No, there's only me," said Joel. "I'm lost."

The man in the dark blue overalls suddenly slapped himself on the forehead.

Joel gave another start.

"Of course," said the man. "They have a meeting. All the local council bosses. I'd forgotten."

The Barefooted Man looked at Joel. He didn't seem in the least unfriendly.

"Did you say you were lost?" he asked. "Who are you looking for?"

"David," said Joel.

"David?" said the Barefooted Man. "You certainly are lost. You'd better come with me. What do you want him for?"

What could Joel say to that?

Now he was in a right mess. The Barefooted Man was blocking the doorway. Joel would never be able to squeeze past him.

The Barefooted Man suddenly smiled broadly. Joel noticed that there were lots of gaps where teeth should have been.

"Of course," said the Barefooted Man. "You're David's kid brother."

"No I'm not," said Joel.

The Barefooted Man didn't hear.

"David's kid brother," he said. "Come with me."

He took hold of Joel's arm and led him away. His grip was not hard and unfriendly. Even so, Joel couldn't wriggle free.

Joel was starting to feel frightened. The Caviar Man might not be at all pleased to find that somebody had turned up claiming to be his younger brother.

"I think he's in here," said the Barefooted Man.

They had descended into a dark basement room, and came to a halt in front of a steel door. Joel could hear a roaring sound behind the door.

The Barefooted Man turned what looked like a motor-car's steering wheel, and the door slid slowly open.

The roaring sound grew louder.

Joel was now beginning to feel scared stiff. Now was the time to run away. But he didn't do so. It was as if he were stuck fast in his own fear.

The Barefooted Man opened the steel door even wider. The noise was overpowering now.

"I think your brother's in here," he yelled, trying to make himself heard above the roaring sound.

Joel suddenly felt very hot. The air flowing out through the steel door was as hot as a summer's day.

"Come on," said the Barefooted Man, propelling Joel in front of him.

Joel stopped dead on the threshold.

The room in front of him was on fire.

Enormous flames were roaring and thundering.

The Barefooted Man was pushing Joel in front of him, straight at the flames.

Joel suddenly remembered his dream.

The dream in which he'd burnt up.

The flames in front of him grew bigger and bigger.

Soon he would be swallowed up by the Underworld....

— SEVEN —

Afterwards, Joel felt a bit silly.

The Barefooted Man no doubt thought that Joel was a relative of Simon Windstorm. The Loonies.

"What the hell do you think you're doing?" the Barefooted Man had shouted. "You're heading straight for the furnace."

Then he'd grabbed Joel by the collar and lifted him to one side.

"If you fall into the furnace, you're a goner," said the Barefooted Man. "Couldn't you see that the doors were open?"

Of course Joel had seen that the doors to the enormous furnace were open. Even so, it felt like standing in front of a hungry beast of prey that had opened its mouth wide and displayed thousands of burning tongues. And Joel had been lured towards them.

"What's the matter with you, lad?" said the Barefooted Man, looking worried. "Has nobody told you that fire is dangerous?"

"Why do you go around in your bare feet?" asked Joel.

Sometimes it was best to answer a question by asking a new one.

"It's so hot here in the boiler room," said the Barefooted Man. "My feet swell up inside my shoes. So I prefer to be barefoot. What's your name, by the way?"

"Samuel," said Joel.

The Barefooted Man smiled.

"David and Samuel," he said. "That really does sound like two brothers."

Joel looked round in the Underworld. The big furnace was in the middle of a gigantic room. Smoke and steam were hissing out of pipes and ventilators.

The beast of the Underworld, Joel thought.

He was being held prisoner here.

"Where does all this heat go to?" he asked. He was forced to shout, in order to be heard. The Barefooted Man was busy throwing big lumps of firewood into the beast's mouth.

"To the hospital and the vicarage and the old people's home and the municipal offices, and lots of other buildings as well," he yelled.

"What's it called?" Joel shouted.

The Barefooted Man straightened his back and wiped the sweat from his brow.

"Called?" he said. "I'm called Nilson."

"I meant the furnace," said Joel.

"Furnaces don't have names," said the Barefooted Man. Then he changed his mind.

"Perhaps you have a suggestion for what we should call it?"

Joel thought for a moment.

The furnace was a sort of dragon. A beast of prey spitting fire.

"Lord of the Fires," he said.

The Barefooted Man nodded.

"A good name," he said. "Lord of the Fires."

Then he threw in some more logs, and closed the big doors. He beckoned Joel to follow him. He led him along winding corridors that followed big pipes, and came to another steel door that he opened by rotating a thick iron handle. The door led into another long corridor, lit up by lamps hanging from the ceiling. It was raw and damp, and Joel wondered why the Barefooted Man's feet didn't seem to be cold.

He stopped.

"Do you know where we are now?" he asked.

Joel shook his head.

"We're underneath the church," said the Barefooted Man. "Right in the middle of the church."

Joel stared up at the ceiling of the stone corridor.

Could that really be possible?

Was the whole church really over his head?

What if the roof fell in?

That would mean he wasn't buried in the churchyard, but in the church itself.

"You don't need to be afraid," said the Barefooted Man. "This corridor isn't going to cave in."

They continued along the corridor, which seemed to be endless. It kept turning at right angles, sometimes sloped downwards, sometimes upwards.

Where are we going? Joel thought.

The Barefooted Man eventually came to a stop at yet another steel door.

SEWER NO. 1 it said on a notice board.

The Barefooted Man opened the door. Joel stepped into a room full of tools and dismantled engines.

"He's not here," said the Barefooted Man.

"That's a pity," said Joel, but he thought it was just as well. It meant his pretending to be the younger brother wouldn't be discovered.

"I expect he's out mending broken pipes," said the Barefooted Man. "But if you like, you can wait in my cabin."

Cabin!

Were there cabins in the Underworld?

Joel had never heard of cabins being anywhere except on a boat.

He followed the Barefooted Man back to where they'd set out from.

"Where are we now?" asked Joel as they turned a corner in the long corridor.

The Barefooted Man smiled.

"Halfway between the shoe shop and Leander's Café," he said.

He pointed to an iron ladder fixed to the stone wall.

"If you climb up there and open the hatch, you'll find yourself outside the café," he said.

This is great, being in the Underworld, Joel thought. Having all those buildings and streets and cars and feet over your head.

David the Caviar Man, who worked down here, must be a good man for Gertrud. Not just for her, but for Joel as well. Joel didn't know anybody else who'd been down here in the underground.

It struck him that he'd have to change the name of his Secret Society.

Now that he was no longer looking for the dog, he ought to give it a different name.

Lords of the Underworld, he thought.

That could be the Caviar Man and me....

"Here's the cabin," said the Barefooted Man, coming to a halt.

They were close to the beast of prey again. Joel could hear the roar.

"I must throw some more wood in," said the Bare-footed Man. "You can wait in there for the time being."

Joel entered the Barefooted Man's cabin. It wasn't a big room, no bigger than an average cellar in a small house. A naked bulb was dangling from a wire in the ceiling. There was a wobbly table and a few ramshackle chairs. The walls were covered in photographs of semi-naked ladies torn out of newspapers and magazines. Joel thought one of them reminded him of Sara. Joel sat down on one of the chairs. As he made himself comfortable, one of the arms fell off. He hurriedly replaced it and moved to another chair. It creaked and squeaked so much that he didn't dare stay on it. Instead he sat down on an upturned beer crate in a corner.

It was very quiet. You couldn't hear the beast through the thick walls and the closed door.

The silence of the Underworld was a new silence for him.

Joel listened. He imagined that the house he lived in with Samuel was directly above his head.

The house that was really a ship straining at its anchor, waiting for wind.

But if the house was a ship, the underground was the bottom of the sea. And Joel was sitting there on an up-turned beer crate. . . .

It was difficult to keep all his thoughts apart.

Joel felt the two one-krona coins in his pocket.

As he fingered them, all the thoughts about anchors and the bottom of the sea faded away.

He stood up and walked round the room. The semi-naked ladies in the torn-out pictures stared at him.

Why hadn't the Barefooted Man come back?

Had the Lord of the Fires gobbled him up?

Joel threw himself at the door like a leopard pouncing on its prey. Perhaps the Barefooted Man had locked him in?

The door was not locked.

Joel opened it slowly and peered out into the corridor.

The steel door to the beast of prey's big hall was ajar.

Joel decided to leave. He didn't need to wait for the Barefooted Man or David any longer. He knew already that David was the right man for Gertrud. He would offer her the Lord of the Underworld as his good deed. How could she possibly object to such a gift?

But perhaps the Barefooted Man would start to wonder if Joel had simply vanished? And David might start asking himself who this unknown younger brother of his was?

Joel opened the door to the Hall of the Beast of Prey. There was a roaring and thundering, and the heat hit him in the face. In the far distance among all the pipes he could see the Barefooted Man throwing logs into the beast's opened mouth.

Just as Joel reached him, the Barefooted Man had thrown in the last of his logs and straightened his back.

"I have to go now," said Joel. "But say hello to David for me. I might come back tomorrow."

The Barefooted Man wiped the sweat off his brow with a snuff-stained handkerchief.

"I didn't know David had a kid brother," he said.

I didn't know I had a big brother either, Joel thought.

"Can you find your own way out?" asked the Barefooted Man.

Joel nodded.

The Barefooted Man opened the heavy door for him. Then he ruffled Joel's hair.

"I can't say you look all that much alike," he said. "David has a mop of fair hair, but your hair is as brown as an old fox's."

"We don't have the same mum," said Joel. "I have to go now."

When he came back to the big entrance hall, it was still empty.

The telephone receiver was still swinging back and forth.

"Bye-bye!" shouted Joel, as loudly as he could.

The sound echoed round the walls.

Then he hurried out to his bicycle.

When he came to Leander's Café, he paused and took a close look at the manhole cover in the street.

He'd been down there. Deep down in the Underworld.

He cycled as fast as he could to the newsstand at the railway station. You could buy packs of pastilles with football pictures in lots of places, but he had more luck when he bought them at the railway station than anywhere else. He hardly ever ended up with flabby wrestlers there.

He bought eight packs of pastilles. He'd never had so many in his hand before. He went into the waiting room and sat down on a bench in a corner. He kept an eye on the ticket window. Stationmaster Knif didn't like people sitting in his waiting room unless they were on their way to somewhere. If you weren't careful, he would sneak up and grab you by the ear.

There was only one other person in the waiting room, apart from Joel. It was an old lady, fast asleep in another corner. Joel was afraid she might start snoring so loudly that Knif would hear her and come to investigate.

Joel opened the first pack. He started by popping a pastille into his mouth. It was yellow, and tasted bitter. Then he carefully extracted the picture card.

A handball player. Gösta Blomgren.

That wasn't anything worth having. Not as bad as a wrestler, but pretty bad even so. Joel only knew two boys who collected handball players.

He stayed calm. He had seven more boxes to open. One handball player wasn't enough to put him into a bad mood. He glanced at the ticket window, then opened the next pack. He swallowed the last of the yellow pastille, and put two new ones into his mouth. There was no need to ration himself. There were at least twenty pastilles in every box. Sometimes there were twenty-two. Once, he'd bought a box containing twenty-four. But there was never less than twenty. He'd been counting and keeping records for several years.

Next picture. An ice hockey player. Anders "Acka" Anderson. He was staring wide-eyed at Joel. Skellefteå ice hockey team, way up north—center forward in the so-called Mosquito Strikers. Joel giggled at the thought of the giant "Acka" shrinking and now popping out of a box of pastilles. He'd been flattened out. Flat Head.

Ice hockey players were OK. It was easy to exchange them for something else. If you had three or four good ice hockey players, you could get a rare footballer. If you had Tumba, you could exchange him for anything you liked—but then, Tumba was probably the most famous ice hockey player ever in Sweden, so that was only fair.

Perhaps box number three would produce the footballer he so badly wanted. Joel's hands were trembling as he opened it. But no! Another ice hockey player, and not only that, but one he'd hardly heard of. This was no good! Still, the next one was bound to contain a footballer. He picked out a red pastille: that was sure to bring him good luck.

As Joel took the picture out of the next box, he held his breath and closed his eyes—but when he opened them he threw the card away in disgust. He didn't even read the name under the pop-eyed face with big ears, it was enough to see that he was a bandy player. Bandy! A sort of poor man's ice hockey! Nobody would want to exchange a footballer for a bandy player.

Things could only get better.

When Joel opened box number five, he got a wrestler. A really flabby wrestler by the name of Arne Turnäs.

Turnip, Joel decided angrily, and popped four pastilles into his mouth.

Still no footballer. His luck had run out. A handball player, two ice hockey players, a bandy-playing idiot and now a wrestler.

Only three boxes left. He ripped open the lids of all three at the same time. Another wrestler! The same wrestler yet again! Turnip! How the hell was that possible? How on earth did they divide up these boxes? Joel shoved a full box of pastilles into his mouth at once, in order to get his own back. Eight boxes and not a single footballer!

The last two were a cyclist and a female fencer. A woman wielding a sword? How could it ever occur to anybody to stuff a woman into a pack of pastilles?

Joel was furious.

He looked at the old woman, fast asleep in the far corner. Her mouth was wide open and her tongue was hanging out.

He tiptoed over to her and put the picture of the female fencer on the old lady's tongue.

Then he ran off and slammed the waiting room door as hard as he could.

On the way to his bike, he glared at the newsstand. If only he could, he'd have ordered the earth to open up and allow the beast of prey down there to swallow up the whole of the stand in one gulp.

It was nearly eleven o'clock. He was hungry. He popped the contents of a full pack of pastilles into his mouth, then set off for home. On the hill down from the Co-op warehouse and the vet's, he let go of the handlebars and closed his eyes. He plucked up enough courage to close his eyes and count up to ten. He had decided that before he was twelve, he would have enough courage to keep his eyes closed and not hold on to the handlebars until he'd counted up to twenty-five.

When he finally stumbled into the kitchen he poured himself a big glass of milk, and emptied all the pastilles he still had left onto the table.

One hundred and twenty-three of them.

If they had been pearls, he'd have been rich.

He scooped the pastilles back into their boxes and put them in the shoe box under his bed. He'd drawn a black skull on that box so that nobody dared open it. A length of cotton hanging down from the lid could easily be a fuse. . . .

When he returned to the kitchen, he noticed that he had a stomachache.

Nothing serious yet. Just something nagging away in the background.

He sat stock-still on the kitchen bench, to see if that

would bring on something more painful. But no: it was still just a nagging ache.

He breathed a sigh of relief. He didn't like the gripes.

Being in pain was painful. If you had a really nasty stomachache, so bad that it brought tears to your eyes, it made the whole of your body hurt. Even the thoughts you had inside your head were painful.

He sat absolutely still, to make sure that the stomachache didn't get worse. He counted slowly to 123. Then he could breathe out again. He wasn't going to get the gripes today.

Nothing could match knowing that you weren't going to be in pain.

He felt inspired to do something useful. Now was the time to work out his strategy.

How could he set up a meeting between Gertrud and the Caviar Man?

He thought again about what he'd read in books about how grown-ups met in order to decide if they ought to get married. But nothing of what he remembered seemed suitable in this case.

Then he thought about Samuel and Mummy Jenny.

They had written letters to each other, Samuel had told him.

Many years ago, his ship had been in dock in Göteborg for repairs. Samuel and some of his shipmates had gone ashore one evening. He'd been walking along the street, stumbled on a paving stone and fallen headlong into the arms of Mummy Jenny.

So that was one way of meeting, and having a son called Joel who experienced a Miracle.

You stumble in the street and fall into somebody.

And then you write letters.

Samuel had told Joel that after Jenny had prevented him from hurting himself on the pavement in Göteborg, he'd persuaded her to give him her address. Then he had written to her from all the foreign ports he'd visited. And in one of the letters they had arranged to meet in Göteborg. In a park, behind a statue.

Joel thought carefully about all this.

He suspected it might be too difficult to arrange for the Caviar Man to stumble on a paving stone and fall headlong into the arms of Gertrud.

So he would have to skip that part out and go straight to the letter stage.

They could send secret letters to each other and arrange a secret meeting. Then no doubt everything would proceed of its own accord.

Secret letters that Joel Gustafson would write.

But how did you write a letter like that? He had no idea.

The library, he thought. There must be a book there about secret letters. A book as important as that had to exist!

He checked the kitchen clock. There were a lot of hours to go yet before Miss Arvidson opened the library. He would have to be patient.

By four o'clock he had only seventy-two pastilles left. He thundered down the stairs and cycled to the library.

Miss Arvidson, the lady in charge of the library, was very strict. She thought that nobody ever borrowed the right books. Moreover, she refused to allow children to borrow the books they wanted. On several occasions Joel had put exciting books about murders and other crimes on her desk, but she had pursed her lips and informed him that those books were for adults only.

Joel couldn't imagine how a book about writing secret letters could be for adults only. Why should anybody have to wait until they were fifteen before learning how to do that?

Nevertheless, he had made up his mind to be cautious. He opened the door quietly, bowed a greeting to Miss Arvidson and took off his dirty boots. Then he went over to the shelves and selected a few religious books. He carried them over to the issue desk.

Miss Arvidson examined the titles and nodded in approval. And started stamping them.

Here we go.

"I'd like to borrow a book about how to write secret letters," Joel said.

Miss Arvidson looked at him in astonishment.

"Secret letters?"

"Love letters," said Joel. "Secret love letters."

Miss Arvidson burst out laughing. It occurred to Joel that he must be the first person in the whole world who had heard Miss Arvidson laughing. Lots of disbelieving faces peered out from among the bookshelves.

Miss Arvidson was howling with laughter.

She laughed so much that Joel started laughing as well. That made her furious.

"That's the silliest thing I've ever heard," she said. "A book about how to write secret letters! Of course there's no such book."

"Love letters," said Joel. "It's not me who wants it, it's my dad."

Involving Samuel was no problem, Joel had decided. He never went near the library anyway.

"If your dad wants to write love letters, he'll have to manage it on his own," said Miss Arvidson. "We have love poems. But not love letters."

"Maybe that would do," said Joel.

Miss Arvidson eyed him up and down, then went to a shelf and returned with two slim volumes.

"These are pretty love poems," she said, and started stamping the books. "But next time he'll have to come and borrow them himself."

Joel cycled back home and put the potatoes on to boil. Then he started reading the thin poetry collections.

They were mostly about roses and thorns. Tears and desperate longing. The word *desperation* came up over and over again.

That would have to do.

When he and Samuel had finished their dinner, he would write the letters.

One letter from Gertrud to the Caviar Man. One letter from the Caviar Man to Gertrud.

He had taken some sheets of letter paper and some envelopes from Samuel's room.

His big plan was ready.

But when he sat in bed after dinner, resting his letter paper on an atlas, it didn't seem so straightforward.

Where should their secret meeting take place?

There wasn't a single statue anywhere in the little town. There wasn't really anywhere that could be called a park. Besides, it had to be a place where Joel could hide nearby and listen to what they said to each other.

He wandered through the whole town in his thoughts. He kept stopping, but failed to find a suitable place.

The churchyard was too spooky after dark.

There were no lights on the football pitch. They wouldn't even be able to find each other.

In the end, just as he was about to give up, he found the solution.

Mr. Under's garden.

It was big, there were lots of trees, and Mr. Under, the horse dealer, had nothing against other people besides himself strolling about in it. There was also a little bird-bath, which was the nearest to a statue you could find in this place.

In addition, Mr. Under wasn't at home. Every autumn he traveled south in order to buy horses.

Joel could hide behind the woodshed. It was only a few meters from there to the birdbath.

So that was that! They'd meet at eight o'clock on Saturday evening.

So now he needed to write the two letters. To make sure the handwriting was different, he wrote Gertrud's letter with his right hand and the Caviar Man's with his left. The one from the Caviar Man was hardest to write: the letters kept wandering off in all directions and he got a cramp in his fingers. But eventually, they were done.

He read through what he had written.

Gertrud's letter first:

"Meet me by the birdbath in the horse dealer's garden at eight o'clock on Saturday evening. If you aren't there, I shall suffer the thorn of despair. A secret admirer."

Joel wasn't sure about the *thorn of despair*. He'd stolen the phrase from one of the poems. But what did it mean? He'd chosen it because the poem was written by a woman.

The letter written by the Caviar Man was longer. Joel assumed that men wrote longer letters than women. But maybe it was the other way round in reality?

"Oh, fondest love of my heart. Meet me at the birdbath at

eight o'clock on Saturday evening. I'm aching to meet you after a thousand years of longing. I kiss your tears. Will you drive me to despair? A secret admirer."

Joel wasn't sure about *fondest*—wouldn't it be better to say *dearest*? But that was what it said in the poem, so no doubt it was right.

He folded the letters and sealed the envelopes.

At that moment, Samuel entered the room.

"Are you writing letters?" he asked.

"I've ordered some catalogs," said Joel.

"I haven't written a letter for ages," said Samuel. Joel thought he sounded sad about that.

"You can write to me," he said. "I promise to answer."

Samuel smiled.

"It's late," he said. "Time to go to bed if you're going to be able to get up for school tomorrow morning."

Joel had intended to take his bike before going to bed, and post the messages in Gertrud's and the Caviar Man's letter boxes. But he was too tired. He'd have to wait until the next day.

It was cold the next evening.

There was a crackling noise from under his tires when Joel set off. He parked his bike by the railway bridge and ran the rest of the way to Gertrud's house. He paused outside the gate. He could see her shadow outlined against the curtains.

So, now I'm going to do my good deed, he thought, and put the letter into the box fastened to the gatepost.

When he came to Lasse the Cabbie's backyard, everything was calm and quiet. Joel had left his bike in a side street, and crept forward cautiously through the shadows. Now he was General Custer's messenger again, sneaking through enemy territory with a message that could mean life or death to the recipient.

There were two letter boxes attached to the fence. He bent down, and managed to make out the names even though the streetlight was a long way away.

Then he slid the letter into the slot.

He had to be certain that he hadn't made a mistake, as the letter box was secured with a little padlock.

So, he'd done it at last!

On Saturday night his good deed would be complete. Then he could concentrate on his geography game. Become a better football player, and find himself a real friend.

He cycled back home. The streets were deserted. He met only one car, outside the Grand Hotel.

He parked his bike in its stand.

Then it dawned on him what he had done.

He froze stiff.

He hadn't written David Lundberg on the envelope.

He'd written the Caviar Man.

"To the Caviar Man from a secret admirer."

How could David know that he was the Caviar Man?

Besides, he might not be too pleased about being compared with caviar.

Damn and blast, Joel thought.

I'm an idiot, idiot, idiot!

Everything is ruined.

He sat down on the freezing-cold steps outside the front door.

How on earth could he have written Caviar Man on the envelope?

How could he possibly have been so stupid?

— EIGHT —

That evening Joel realized that there is no anger greater than the anger you direct at yourself.

He had never been so furious with himself as he was now.

Even his father wondered what was the matter with him.

"What are you wandering around and muttering at?" he asked.

"I'm swearing," said Joel.

Samuel looked at him in surprise.

"Why?"

"Why not?" said Joel.

"There's usually a reason for swearing," said Samuel. "I swear when I stumble in the forest. Or twist my ankle. Or hit myself on the thumb."

"I've hit myself on the head," said Joel.

Samuel looked worried.

"Have you fallen off your bike?" he asked.

"I've hit myself inside my head," said Joel.

Then he went to his room and slammed the door behind him.

Samuel could see it was best to leave Joel in peace. He went back to his armchair and continued reading the newspaper.

Joel got his own back on himself by eating all the pastilles he had left. All seventy-two of them. If he got a stomachache as a result, that would serve him right for being so stupid as to write the Caviar Man on the letter to David.

Thoughtlessness, that's what it was. He'd learnt that from Miss Nederström. If you did something stupid, you were thoughtless.

It was a good word. It meant that your head was empty. Your skull was no more than a tin can on which there happened to be a pair of blue eyes, a nose and a mouth. And tousled hair. A rusty tin can by the name of Joel Gustafson. A rusty, thoughtless tin can.

Of course David wouldn't go to the birdbath on Saturday evening. He would read the letter twenty times without understanding a thing. Then he'd tear it into little pieces and throw it into the wastepaper basket. At best he would forget all about it. At worst, he would start thinking. No doubt the Barefooted Man had told him about the peculiar kid brother who'd paid a visit to the Underworld. He would realize right away that it was an imposter. Then he would start searching the town for him.

It was clear to Joel that he would have to change his appearance. Dress up as somebody else. But what would he say when Miss Nederström asked him why he looked different? What would Samuel say? And his classmates?

And Otto! Needless to say, Otto would put two and two together. Nobody was as good as Otto when it came to ferreting out facts. He'd tip off the Caviar Man, Joel would be captured and thrown into the jaws of the beast of prey. He would be a human sacrifice in the mouth of the Lord of the Fires.

Joel went to the kitchen and tried to change his appearance in the cracked shaving mirror. He sprinkled water onto his hair and tried to make a parting. But his hair just stood on end, no matter how wet he made it. Water ran down inside his shirt collar and formed pools on the floor. He put on his father's spare pair of reading glasses that he found on a shelf. But no matter how hard he tried, they simply slid down his nose the moment he moved.

You ought to be able to change your sex, he thought. One day Joel, the next Joella.

He stood in the doorway of Samuel's room.

"When will my beard start to grow?" he asked.

Samuel lowered his newspaper and stared at him in surprise.

125

"Why do you ask that?"

"I just wondered."

"You'll have to wait for a few years yet," said Samuel, returning to his newspaper. "Think yourself lucky. You don't have to worry about getting shaved."

"I'm going to grow a long beard," said Joel. "I'm never going to shave."

He went back to his room.

There was nothing he could do.

His big plan was in ruins.

Not even General Custer could help him. When he stood before the strict general and tried to explain how he had lost the letter containing the vital information, he couldn't think of anything to say.

The general passed sentence on the spot. Joel would be shot at dawn, when the first rays of sun turned the prairie red. . . .

And all this was due to him for not looking both ways before running across the street outside the bar. If Eklund had only turned up ten seconds sooner or ten seconds later, nothing would have happened.

Joel used to think that what made a day exciting was when something unexpected happened. Now he wasn't so sure anymore. You ought to know about some events before they happened. And you should also be able to forbid certain things from happening.

He wondered if he ought to say a prayer.

Not because he thought it would help. But there was

no harm in trying. Perhaps Miracle People had certain rights that other people didn't have?

He put his hands together and mumbled a prayer, as fast as he could.

"Dear God, please make the Caviar Man come to the bird-bath on Saturday. Amen."

He regretted it immediately.

Perhaps God didn't like the idea of people who didn't really believe in him saying prayers. Maybe it was a bit like cheating when you were playing cards?

There was nothing he could do.

He went into Samuel's room. His dad had taken off his socks and was clipping his toenails.

"Are you still wandering around and swearing?" Samuel asked.

"No," said Joel. "But I want to tell you something I want for my twelfth birthday."

"Are you really going to be twelve next?" said Samuel. "Good heavens, but time flies!"

"Can I?"

"Ask for whatever you want. As long as it's not too expensive."

"It costs nothing," said Joel.

"Good," said Samuel. "What do you want?"

"I want us to move," said Joel. "Now. Soon."

Samuel stopped clipping his toenails and eyed Joel up and down.

"To the sea," said Joel. "I want you to become a

sailor again, and to take me with you. I want us to move now."

"Not until you've finished school," said Samuel. "Then we can move, perhaps. But not before."

"I've learnt enough," said Joel. "I want us to move now."

Samuel gave him a searching look.

"Has something happened to make you want to move now?" he asked.

Joel very nearly came out with the truth. Explained everything that had happened. But something stopped him. He didn't want to reveal what a thoughtless rusty tin can he really was. Maybe Samuel might say it was impossible to take such an empty-headed fool with him to sea? He couldn't afford to risk that.

"Nothing has happened," said Joel. "Nothing ever happens here, except when I get run over by the Ljusdal bus."

"That's not something to joke about," said Samuel. His voice was suddenly as sharp as Miss Nederström's.

Joel didn't like that voice. It frightened him.

"It doesn't matter," said Joel. "Of course we'll have to wait until I've finished school before we move."

"Exactly," said Samuel. "Then we shall see."

His voice was back to normal again now. A bit rough and hoarse. Just as Joel was used to hearing it.

Joel got undressed and settled down in bed.

In order not to think about the Caviar Man and the letter, he decided he would tell himself a story. He searched his brain for stories he'd started before but never finished.

There was one about how he was looking for a secret tree in the depths of the forest, not far from Four Winds Lake. A map was buried at the foot of this tree. If he found it, he'd be able to sail to the Forgotten Island. A big island somewhere in the Indian Ocean. An island that could only be found by somebody who had the map.

That was a good story. It could have no end of endings.

When Samuel had been in to say good night, Joel curled up and closed his eyes. Now he was no longer in bed. It was a summer's morning, soon after school had broken up. He was sitting in the front seat, next to Simon Windstorm, and they were on their way to Four Winds Lake. Simon didn't smell foul any longer. He was newly bathed and perfectly clean. He would soon stop the lorry and drop Joel off. Joel had to look for the secret tree by himself. Simon was merely his chauffeur. He obeyed Joel's slightest gesture. The window was open and a butterfly started flying in circles round Joel's face. It was no ordinary butterfly. Joel soon discovered that the pattern on its wings was not a haphazard mixture of colors. There was a message written on those wings. A mysterious message indicating where he should go in order to find the secret tree. Joel followed every movement the butterfly made. The message on its wing was beginning to make sense....

Joel fell asleep.

The Caviar Man couldn't reach Joel in his dreams. Big swarms of butterflies kept watch over Joel's slumber.

Samuel tiptoed into the dark room and tucked Joel in.

Then he left the kitchen door ajar so that a narrow strip of light wandered over the floor and settled on Joel's face.

A few days later, it was Saturday.

Joel woke up early. Despite not having been woken up by anybody.

He knew straightaway that it was Saturday, and that he didn't have to go to school.

He pulled the covers over his head, and tried to imagine that it was Sunday instead. That Saturday had never existed. A day that was missed out, and nobody noticed. But when Samuel started clattering about with the coffeepot in the kitchen, it was still Saturday. Joel sat up.

What the hell am I going to do? he thought.

Shall I go there tonight, and hide behind the woodshed?

Or shall I just forget all about it?

He tumbled out of bed and got dressed. There were holes in his underpants, and in one of his socks. When he raised the blind, he saw that it was frosty outside again. Red leaves seemed to glow against the white background.

There was a mumbling and bumbling coming from the kitchen.

Samuel was trying to button up his shirt.

He and Sara were going off in a car today. They were

going to visit a friend of Samuel's who was celebrating his fortieth birthday. Samuel had borrowed a car from Nyberg, the bouncer. Sara had fixed it. The intention was that Joel should go as well, but he said that he'd prefer to stay at home. He still hadn't been able to make up his mind whether he should hide behind the woodshed in horse dealer Under's garden, or not. He'd done everything he could think of in order to help himself reach a decision. He'd tried drawing the shortest straw—if he drew the short one three times in succession, he would hide behind the woodshed. If not, he would forget about it. He'd borrowed Samuel's pack of cards and tried cutting in various ways in order to decide. At least four cards out of ten had to be spades. In that case he'd hide behind the woodshed. But that didn't work either. He'd tried counting paving stones and jumping over the cracks, but that didn't help. And so he told Samuel that he'd prefer to stay at home.

"I'm busy inventing a game," he told Samuel. "I thought I'd take it to school on Monday and show it to Miss Nederström."

Sara had made him some pancakes. They were on a dish in the pantry. They were to make up for his not being able to have a slice or two of birthday cake.

"Come and help me with my tie," shouted Samuel from the kitchen.

It was the blue tie. The sailor's tie. The one Samuel had bought in Glasgow. The silk tie. Joel knelt on a chair and tied the complicated knot for his father. Samuel smelt of aftershave. He was humming away as he bent his head back to make it easier for Joel to tie the knot.

"Thank you," Samuel said when the knot was finished.

"Pocket money," said Joel.

"Haven't you had it already?" asked Samuel with a frown.

It was the same every Saturday. Haven't you had your pocket money already? Then he smiled and took out his purse and gave Joel one krona.

Joel went out with Samuel to watch him drive off in Nyberg's car. It wasn't a very special car. Not like the Pontiac Joel had seen in Krage's showrooms. It was a DKW that rattled and spluttered like a motorbike. It was green, with a white roof.

"It's a nice car," Samuel said.

"A Pontiac would be better," said Joel.

Samuel gave him a look, then burst out laughing.

"Don't be silly!" he said. "Who can afford a Pontiac? Only the rich."

We are so poor that we can't even afford a DKW, Joel thought.

But then he regretted thinking such a thing. He could see how happy Samuel was at the prospect of going out in a car with Sara, even if it was only a borrowed car.

"Don't do anything silly while we're away," said Samuel, who had already sat down behind the wheel.

I've already done something silly, Joel thought.

"Of course not," he said.

"I won't be late," said Samuel. "But don't sit up waiting for me."

Then he engaged the gear and drove off. Joel waved. Then he went back up to the kitchen and ate one of the cold pancakes. He got out the jars of lingonberry jam and cloudberry jam and some cream and some sugar. He spread double layers of everything onto the pancake and rolled it up. If Samuel had seen it he would have been annoyed— but Joel didn't have a guilty conscience. After all, Samuel was going to be eating birthday cake all day.

Joel counted the pancakes. There were eight of them. He'd already eaten one. He'd have two for lunch. And save the rest for dinner.

The only question was: would he be able to wait until lunch before eating the next one?

As a reward for not eating a second pancake now, he gave himself two spoonfuls of jam. When he returned the jars of jam to the pantry, he quickly unscrewed the lid of the cloudberry jam jar and took another spoonful.

The day passed slowly. He took out one of Samuel's rolled-up sea charts, the one showing the east coast of Africa and the islands of the Indian Ocean. He tried to work out where the secret island might be. He searched for a spot where the sea was very deep, and it was a long way away from both Africa and India.

Suddenly a dead fly fell down from the lamp shade and onto the map. It landed on a spot where the sea was three

133

thousand meters deep. Joel imagined the long journey down to the bottom of the sea.

Then he rolled up the chart again.

The day passed very slowly.

And he still hadn't made up his mind whether to hide behind the woodshed or not.

He gave himself an order to make up his mind no later than two o'clock. Four hours to go. He couldn't wait any longer than that.

The one-krona coin was on the kitchen table in front of him. He'd be able to spin it if necessary and choose heads or tails.

But three o'clock came round, and four, and five, and he still hadn't made up his mind. He ate the pancakes that were almost bursting with cream and jam. He shifted the furniture round in his room, and moved the bed so that he'd be lying with his feet towards the window and the blinds. He spent half an hour trying to roll up the blind using only his foot.

It was dark outside already.

I won't bother, he thought. I'll forget all about those letters.

But at seven o'clock he went out even so. He had eaten the last of the pancakes, and the jar of cloudberry jam was empty.

A noisy car packed with teenagers thundered past. The backseat was lit up by a red lamp. A fox's tail was attached to the radio aerial. It was a Chevrolet, he noticed.

Black, with shiny chrome. A portable gramophone on the shelf in the back window was blaring out music. Elvis.

There was a noisy group of people outside the Grand Hotel. Joel recognized Mr. Waltin, editor of the local newspaper that came out once a week. Mr. Waltin had been on safari in Africa. Now he wrote about boring meetings and logjams in the river. But that man had been to Africa. He had been under the same hot sun that had also heated up Samuel. . . .

Just past the Co-op was a green-painted block of flats. Joel could hear voices arguing through an open window. As he couldn't see any faces, it was the voices that were arguing. They rose and fell and nattered away at each other like monkeys in a treetop.

Joel could see the face of the church clock, gleaming yellow. Nearly half past seven.

He walked along the path that meandered between the river and the vicarage. When he got to the back of Mr. Under's house, he paused and listened. There was a rustling sound behind him. A cat? No, just a wood mouse. Then everything was quiet again. The stars were glittering in a clear sky. He climbed over the fence and groped his way forward between the rows of currant bushes. Now he could see the birdbath lit up by a not very bright lamp. Nobody was there yet. Red leaves were floating in the cloudy water of the birdbath. He hurried over to the woodshed and tried to melt into the shadow. He stumbled into a broken sleigh and staggered slightly from the impact. More rustling around his feet. Lots of mice were making their way towards the houses. That was what happened every autumn. And it was autumn now. He could feel that the air he was breathing was cool.

The church clock in the distance chimed three times: a quarter of an hour left.

Nobody will come, he thought. Not the Caviar Man, not Gertrud either.

He suddenly felt scared. What if they realized that he was the one who had written the letters! Gertrud might never let him into her house again.

Can good deeds be turned into evil deeds?

He heard a crunching noise coming from the gravel path leading from the main road. That wasn't a mouse. Those were footsteps. There was somebody coming.

A black shadow glided past the birdbath.

Joel couldn't believe his eyes.

It was Miss Nederström! What was she doing here?

Joel got ready to run away.

But Miss Nederström didn't stop at the birdbath. She kept on walking and disappeared into the shadows. Her footsteps died away. Joel remembered that she had a sister who lived on the other side of the river. Perhaps she was on her way there, and had taken a shortcut through the horse dealer's garden?

He suppressed a giggle. Miss Nederström taking a shortcut! Perhaps she climbed over fences as well....

The clock struck eight. Joel counted the chimes to be certain. . . . Seven, eight.

The red leaves were still floating in the birdbath.

Nobody. Nobody at all. Joel was the only one who had turned up.

It was cold behind the woodshed. Mice were scuttling around through the fallen leaves. There was one mouse in particular that was scratching away at the other gable end of the woodshed. Scratching and scratching away.

Then it coughed. It cleared its throat.

It wasn't a mouse at all. There was somebody standing there, at the other gable end of the woodshed. Somebody who was hiding, just like Joel was.

Joel closed his eyes, in the hope that it would make him even more invisible. What he really wanted to do was to run away. But his fear paralyzed him.

There was a crunching noise from the gravel path again. The footsteps were coming from the side facing the river. They were getting closer.

Then they fell silent. There was no coughing from the other end of the woodshed either. Joel hardly dared to breathe. Who was it, hiding behind the other end of the woodshed?

Now the footsteps were approaching again. It was Gertrud. She was moving very cautiously, as if she'd rather not be there at all. Joel wanted to shout out and run to greet her. He wanted to tell her that there was somebody behind the other end of the woodshed. Then the pair of them would run away, along the riverbank, over the railway bridge, and they wouldn't stop until they were in Gertrud's kitchen. It would be warm and light there. Maybe Gertrud would fetch her trombone and play a tune for him?

Joel could see Gertrud standing at the very edge of the area illuminated by the lamp. He could see that she had put on her very best clothes. The hole she had instead of a nose was plugged with a silk handkerchief. Joel knew she never used that normally.

The church clock chimed once again. A quarter past eight. Gertrud looked round.

The Caviar Man isn't going to turn up, Joel thought.

Then the penny dropped.

It was the Caviar Man hiding behind the woodshed, of course. Spying on Gertrud.

Joel was furious. Even though he was the one who had set it all up, he felt sorry for Gertrud. She wasn't somebody people were allowed to spy on.

Now the rustling sound started again. It was getting nearer. And nearer. Joel crouched down next to the broken sleigh. He hardly dared to breathe.

A shadow passed in front of him.

How could you see a shadow when everything was black?

Then he heard a whisper.

"That bloody noseless hag."

That was all. The shadow vanished silently in among the currant bushes.

Gertrud was standing there motionless, waiting.

The clock chimed again. Twice. Half past eight.

Then she left. Joel could see that her head was bowed. She was disappointed. Her footsteps sounded sad. They faded away, and she was gone.

Joel ran through the garden like a madman. He had to get away from there. He ran all the way home. When he fumbled for the door key under Samuel's boots on the landing, he was so out of breath that he could hardly stand up. His legs were shaking.

He switched on every light in the flat. He wanted to get rid of the darkness.

I've hurt Gertrud, he thought.

How could it turn out like that?

He went to the pantry and ate some more jam. He shoveled it into himself, spoonful after spoonful.

Then he went to the kitchen and examined himself in the cracked shaving mirror.

The Miracle Man, Joel Gustafson.

"What should I do now?" he asked his reflection.

What should I do now?

Then he thought he could see Gertrud's face in the mirror.

She looked very sad.

All alone in her kitchen. On the other side of the river...

— NINE —

Some days could be worse than others.

But Joel couldn't remember ever experiencing one like this.

Absolutely everything went wrong.

It started in the morning as he was getting ready to leave for school. He couldn't find one of his Wellingtons. He looked everywhere, but there was no sign of it. How on earth can a Wellington boot disappear? And why only one? He conducted another search, and even looked in the pantry. But no luck. He could see from the kitchen clock that if he didn't find it within the next minute, he would be late for school.

But no Wellington. It had vanished without trace.

So he put on his shoes instead and started to tie the laces. No problem with the left one, but the lace in the right shoe snapped. No doubt a mouse had been nibbling at it. He swore and tugged at the lace, cut it with a pair of scissors and tried to thread it through the eyelets, but of course they were too small. The kitchen clock seemed to be going faster than before—the hands were racing round.

And needless to say, he was late for school. Otto sat at his desk, smirking at him. Miss Nederström told him to come out to the front and explain why he was late.

"My shoelace broke," he said.

The class started laughing, and he had to admit that it sounded silly. So silly that he started giggling himself. Everybody was laughing, apart from Miss Nederström. Nothing made her more angry than laughter. Joel had noted that down in his logbook, on the page where he listed all the strange things that grown-ups do. Getting angry with people who laugh . . .

Joel tried to save the situation by explaining that one of his Wellingtons had vanished. But that only made Miss Nederström even more annoyed.

"Go and sit down, Joel Gustafson," she said. "If you carry on arriving late like this, I'll have to have a word with your father."

She's forgotten about the Miracle, Joel thought. If I'd said I was late because of the Miracle, she wouldn't have been angry, I'm sure.

The day had begun badly, but things were going to get worse. Joel had forgotten all about the geography

141

homework they'd been set. That was his best subject, and the one he found most fun. He was top of the class in geography. Nobody knew as much about foreign countries and oceans as he did. But today's lesson wasn't about foreign countries: it was about Sweden. Joel didn't know all that much about Sweden. He ought to have read up on what was set, and consulted his atlas. But he'd forgotten. He tried to look confident, as if he knew the answers to all Miss Nederström's questions. He nodded when one of his classmates answered a question correctly. He hoped she would think that he knew all the answers, as usual. But then she surprised him with a question directed at him. Just as if she had been a hawk, and he had been a dove.

"I didn't hear the question," said Joel. He had heard, in fact. *What is the town of Örebro famous for?* He didn't know. He needed to think about it.

Miss Nederström repeated the question.

His classmates eyed him in anticipation. Joel could feel Otto smirking behind his back.

He thought as hard as he could. Örebro? He couldn't even remember where the place was. Örebro, Örebro...

He suddenly remembered one of the pictures in one of the eight packs of pastilles he'd bought. Wasn't one of the wrestlers from Örebro?

"Well," said Miss Nederström. "Are you going to answer or not?"

"Örebro has one of Sweden's foremost wrestling clubs," said Joel.

The class exploded with laughter. Miss Nederström turned white in the face with anger.

"You are insubordinate, Joel Gustafson," she said. "Of course you know that Örebro is famous for its shoe-making industry. You ought to have thought about that this morning when your shoelace snapped. But you don't want to answer the question. You just want to annoy me, Joel Gustafson."

"I didn't mean that at all," said Joel.

Miss Nederström had marched up to his desk. She grabbed hold of his ear and twisted it. Her fingers were like talons. She twisted so hard that he had tears in his eyes.

"Let that be a lesson to you," she said, going back to her desk.

Joel was staring hard at his desk lid. There was nothing so unpleasant as having your ear twisted. It was worse than dreaming that you'd been burnt alive. Joel was furious. But he was ashamed as well. And it hurt.

And Otto sat there behind him, smirking. Joel would never be able to lift his gaze from the lid of his desk. He would sit staring at the lid of his desk until he grew old and fell onto the floor and died.

That's how it felt. Deep down Joel knew that it would pass, and he would forget about it. Everything passed eventually. But just now, that's not how it felt. Just now he felt petrified. Like the petrified prince in a fairy story, who would have to sit there staring at his desk lid for a thousand years...

When the bell rang, he was the last one to leave the room. The others were standing outside the door, waiting for him. They were all smirking. Otto was at the front of them, smirking more than anybody else. Joel forced himself to stare right through his classmates. He wasn't Joel any longer. He was on his way to his own execution. General Custer hadn't been able to save him. Joel had shot the drunken Lieutenant Hickock. It was self-defense. But there were no witnesses. Now Joel was going to be hanged. The gallows had already been raised on the hill outside the palisade. The drums were rolling. But Joel was icy calm. He stared right through all the people who were staring at him. He would die with dignity. He wasn't the one who was frightened. It was the people watching him who were frightened. He walked resolutely up to the noose. The hangman wanted to tie a cloth over his eyes. But Joel shook his head. Then he smiled. He was calm. He would die calmly and with dignity. They would write songs about how calm he was. How brave. And then everybody would realize that he was innocent. General Custer would assemble the whole regiment and reveal the terrible truth—that Joel Gustafson was innocent. The fort would be renamed in his honor. Just now it was called Fort Jameson. In future it would be known as Fort Joel. The hangman placed the noose around Joel's neck, and Joel gazed calmly over the heads of the assembled multitude. Then he fell, and was dead. But he could still see. The screaming masses gaping at his body dangling from the gallows. He could still see.

The bell rang and break was over. Joel still stared right through his classmates. He'd carry on staring through them all day....

At last school was over. Joel took a long route home in order to avoid his classmates. He walked by the side of the wall behind the churchyard. Then he noticed that one of the big entrance doors to the church was half open. Without really knowing why, he walked up to the door and peered inside. It was dark in the church. He sneaked through the door. He listened. Not a sound to be heard. He moved silently among the pews. Right at the front was the tall altarpiece. It was as if he had always used to sit there and look at it after school. He didn't like the painting. When he was younger he used to be frightened of it. It depicted Jesus on the point of flying up to heaven. He was hanging in the air, a meter or so above the ground. A Roman soldier was kneeling in front of Jesus. He was wearing a helmet, but had dropped his sword. Jesus was all white, but the Roman soldier was dark. Behind them, a storm was whipping up. The clouds were pitch-black.

Joel went up to the altar rail. He'd never been as close to the picture as this before. It looked even bigger now. It was growing. And the thunderstorm was approaching. The dark clouds were growing bigger and bigger.

The thunder resounded with a frightening roar. Joel gave a start, as if he'd been struck by lightning. The thundery roar echoed between the walls of the murky church.

Then it dawned on him that it wasn't thunder at all, but that somebody had started to play the organ at the back of the church, upstairs. He realized that somebody was practicing, starting again from the beginning. It must have been Oliver Organ rehearsing for the next service. The organist was a hunchback, and was so nearsighted that his glasses had treble lenses.

Joel sat at the end of a pew and listened. Oliver Organ kept repeating sections over and over again. It was powerful and beautiful and frightening. Joel looked down at the floor, and remembered that he had been in the Underworld. He had carried the whole of this church on his shoulders. He'd been so deep down that the roar of the organ couldn't penetrate.

His mind was racing. That accursed town of Örebro. And the Caviar Man, who had disappointed Gertrud.

I must do something else, Joel thought. I can't let it finish like this.

The Caviar Man must realize that Gertrud was the best wife he could possibly find. Where did it say that every person had to have a nose? You could still breathe without one. Oliver Organ was a hunchback, but he played the organ better than anybody else. The Caviar Man must realize that the nose Gertrud didn't have made her special . . .

Joel listened to the organ. This time Oliver Organ played a whole piece through without stopping.

Music, Joel thought. Kringström's orchestra played at the dances held in the Community Center on Saturday nights. That's where the Caviar Man and Gertrud will meet. I'll write some new letters. I'll let Gertrud send him a present. It was a mistake to arrange the meeting by the birdbath in the horse dealer's garden.

It was good to think about Gertrud and the Caviar Man. When he did, he could no longer feel Miss Nederström's talons twisting his ear. It was good to think about something completely different.

He went back to school and collected his bike. He'd forgotten about it.

How could you forget your bike? It was just as peculiar as a Wellington boot vanishing.

When he got home, he found the missing Wellington straightaway. It had been covered up by some firewood that Samuel had carried in last night. Joel picked the boot up and threw it at the wall. He was really throwing it at Miss Nederström's bottom.

The next time she twists my ear, I'll do the same back to her.

I shall start a Secret Society devoted to doing away with all ear twisters.

Down with Ear Twisters!

He borrowed some more letter paper from Samuel's room. When he settled down on his bed to write, he realized that he couldn't remember if he had written to Gertrud or to the Caviar Man with his left hand. It took him ages to remember which one it was.

This time he'd write the letters without first looking through the books of poetry he'd borrowed from the library.

"*Meet me at the dance in the Community Center on Saturday,*" he had the Caviar Man write to Gertrud. "*I was prevented from coming the other day,*" he added after a moment's hesitation. He wasn't sure how he should sign the letter. In the end he decided to write "*Your beloved.*"

He sealed the envelope and wrote "*Gertrud.*"

Her surname was Håkanson, but he didn't add that. The first name was enough.

Before he wrote Gertrud's letter to the Caviar Man, he needed to gather strength. He drank some milk and made two big sandwiches. The level of jam in the pots had sunk worryingly over the past few days. He had to make do with a few slices of sausage instead.

Then he went to Samuel's room and started looking for a present for Gertrud to give to the Caviar Man. Something in Samuel's wardrobe that he never used and so would never miss.

Mummy Jenny's dress was hanging in there.

Come back, Joel thought. Come back and fetch your dress. Come back and tell us why you went away. Why we weren't good enough, Samuel and me . . .

He let go of the dress. Today was not a good day to see it hanging in Samuel's wardrobe. To touch it, feel it.

He carried on searching. Eventually he found a tie he had never seen Samuel wearing. It was green. The Caviar Man could have it. Samuel would never notice that it wasn't there.

Joel sat at the kitchen table and started to make an envelope that would be big enough for both a letter and a tie. He opened out a small envelope to see how it was put together. Then he cut out and glued a bigger envelope from a sheet of brown wrapping paper. Bits of white glue stuck to the paper and the edges were not quite straight, but it would have to do. Besides, he didn't have any more wrapping paper.

Then he wrote the letter from Gertrud to the Caviar Man.

"I'll be at the Community Center on Saturday night. I hope you like the tie. I bought it in Hull. Your beloved."

Joel checked one of Samuel's sea charts to see how the town of Hull was spelt. Joel knew for certain that Samuel had once bought a hat there. So it must be possible to buy a tie there as well. There can't be Hat Towns and Tie Towns, he thought. And how could the Caviar Man know if Gertrud had been to Hull or not? If that's a problem after they are married, they'll have to sort it out by themselves.

"I can't do everything!" Joel shouted into the empty kitchen.

They'd have to do *something* themselves!

He put the tie and the letter into the envelope.

When it came to writing the name on the envelope, he very nearly made the same mistake again. Nearly put the Caviar Man instead of David.

But he wrote: *"Mr. David Lundberg."*

That was that. Later on he would put the letters in the appropriate letter boxes.

He peeled the potatoes, filled a pan with water and sat down at the kitchen table to keep an eye on them and make sure they didn't boil over. Between then and Saturday there was a big problem he had to solve. How was he going to be able to get into the Community Center and make sure that Gertrud and the Caviar Man really did meet? He'd have to find some way of sneaking inside and hiding. But how would he be able to manage that?

The next day everything was back to normal at school. Miss Nederström was in a good mood, and everybody seemed to have forgotten that the previous day she had twisted Joel's ear. Moreover, Otto was ill, so Joel didn't have to put up with his sneering face.

After school Joel cycled to the Community Center. He rode round the building five times, trying to find a good solution to his problem.

What would Geronimo have done? Joel wondered. How would he have tricked his way into the fort?

Joel tried to think the way Geronimo would have

thought. If it had been a question of defending the fort, he would have tried to think his way into General Custer's mind. Indians were best at capturing forts, but the white soldiers were best at defending them.

What would Geronimo have done?

Joel dismounted and studied the fort. The Community Center Fort. In the display cases outside the entrance were film posters. Just now there was a romantic film running, starring Vivien Leigh and Gary Cooper. Joel imagined Vivien Leigh without a nose, and Gary Cooper with blond hair like the Caviar Man. Then the film could have been about Gertrud and the Caviar Man.

A notice in the next display case announced that Kringström's orchestra would be playing at the dance on Saturday evening.

That gave Joel his idea.

Kringström would help Joel to get into the Community Center Fort.

Joel knew that Kringström lived in the same block of flats as the Greyhound, Eva-Lisa. She had told Joel that when Kringström wasn't performing somewhere with his orchestra, all he did was listen to gramophone records. He used to play them so loudly that all his neighbors had complained. So he had built a room inside a room so that no noise could escape through the walls of his flat.

Kringström played the clarinet and saxophone. But if anybody in his orchestra was ill, he could stand in for them and play any instrument you liked.

A brilliant idea occurred to Joel.

Not even Geronimo could have thought of a better plan!

Joel cycled up the hill to the block of flats where Kringström lived. As he didn't want the Greyhound to see him and start asking awkward questions, Joel sneaked in through the back door as quickly as he could. Kringström lived on the ground floor. Joel rang the bell. But perhaps Kringström was in his soundproof room listening to gramophone records? If no sound could leak out of there, perhaps no sound could get in either? Such as the door-bell. Joel rang again. Should he hammer on the door instead? Perhaps the neighbors would come to investigate and wonder what was going on? He rang once more. The door opened, and Kringström appeared, in dressing gown and slippers, even though it was late afternoon.

"Ah, good afternoon," said Joel. "I'd like to speak to Mr. Kringström, please."

Kringström adjusted his glasses, which had been up on his forehead, and eyed Joel up and down.

"I don't want to buy anything," he said.

"I'm not selling anything," said Joel. "I want to learn to play the saxophone."

"You don't say," said Kringström. "The saxophone? Not the guitar, like everybody else?"

"No," said Joel. "I want to learn to play the saxophone."

"Well, I never!" said Kringström. "Come in so that I can have a good look at you!"

He stepped to one side and ushered Joel in.

Joel knew that Kringström lived alone. He had been married and divorced lots of times. He had a reputation of being a womanizer, even though he was over fifty and nearly bald. It was even said that he'd had a relationship with the scary Eulalia Mörker.

But now he lived alone again. Joel entered the flat and had the impression he was in a music shop. There were gramophone records everywhere. Mainly 78s in brown covers. But there were also some LPs and some little EPs. The walls were covered in shelves. Where there were no records, there were instrument cases. Joel followed Kringström into another room—and here was the room within a room. In the middle of the floor, like a ticket office. No windows. Just a door. Kringström removed a pile of records from a chair and invited Joel to sit down.

Joel told him his name. He tried to be as polite as he possibly could.

"The saxophone, eh?" said Kringström, scratching his nose. "Why don't you want to learn how to play the guitar like everybody else?"

"I think the saxophone sounds best," said Joel. "Almost like an organ."

Kringström nodded.

"And you want me to teach you, is that it?" he asked.

"Yes," said Joel.

Kringström sighed.

"I don't have the time," he said. "But I think I'm the only person in this dump who can play the saxophone."

"We don't need to start right away," said Joel. "I don't think I can afford a saxophone yet."

Kringström flung out his arms.

"You can borrow a saxophone from me," he said. "But I don't know if I can teach you, even though I play it myself."

Kringström reached down to pick up the shiny golden saxophone lying on the floor beside him.

He handed it to Joel.

"Blow!" he said. "See if you can get a sound out of it!"

Joel raised the mouthpiece to his lips and blew. All that came out was a hissing sound. He tried again, blew as hard as he could. Now there was a little squeak, as if somebody had stood on a cat's tail.

Kringström shook his head.

"Give it to me," he said.

And he played. The tune resounded round the room. The windowpanes rattled. Notes ran up and down, as if they were racing up and down stairs.

Somebody banged loudly on one of the walls. Kringström stopped playing immediately.

"They don't understand music," he said sadly.

"We could practice round at my place," said Joel. "The woman who lives below us is nearly deaf."

"I'll think it over," said Kringström. "We don't need to decide anything here and now."

Now came the crucial moment. Joel would have to ask the most important question.

"Could I perhaps sit behind the orchestra and listen?" he asked. "When the orchestra's performing?"

"Of course you can," said Kringström. "But we shan't be performing until Saturday."

"Yes, at the Community Center," said Joel. "Could I sit behind you and listen then?"

Kringström smiled.

"If you help us to carry the instruments in," he said.

"When do you want me to be there?" Joel asked. He could feel his face flushing. His plan had succeeded!

"Come to the back door at half past seven," said Kringström. "But you'll have to go now. I must go back to Paradise."

Paradise? It was only when Kringström pointed at the little soundproof room that the penny dropped.

"That's my Paradise," said Kringström. "In there, there's nothing but music. And me."

Joel cycled home. Geronimo Gustafson had carried out the first stage of the big plan. On Saturday he would capture the fort.

He thought about Kringström and his Paradise.

He pictured himself fixing posters in the display cabinet outside the Community Center. Joel Gustafson's Orchestra would play at a dance. . . .

Now he was no longer wearing his baggy jacket. Now he was in a shiny silver blazer. And white shoes. He was beating time and directing the orchestra. Emblazoned on the side of the big bass drum it said JGO in highly decorated letters. Joel Gustafson's Orchestra.

For the rest of the evening he couldn't get out of his head what was going to happen on Saturday night.

He went to Samuel's room. His dad was reading the newspaper and listening to the sound of the sea on the radio.

"Can you dance?" he asked.

Samuel lowered the newspaper.

"Of course I can dance," he said in surprise. "Can't everybody?"

"I can't," Joel said.

"You'll learn before long," said Samuel. "Can't Eva-Lisa teach you?"

"But you never dance," said Joel.

"Do you want me to dance here in the kitchen?" asked Samuel, with a laugh.

The next question came tumbling out of Joel's mouth, without his having thought about it in advance.

"What about Mummy Jenny?" he said. "Did you dance with her? Did you dance together?"

"I suppose we did," Samuel said. Joel could see a shadow of unrest settling over his face.

He wished he hadn't asked the question. Where did it come from? It simply jumped out, as if it had been hiding inside there and waiting for Joel to open his mouth.

The unrest faded away. Samuel was back to normal.

"Maybe we should," he said. "Maybe I should invite Sara to go dancing with me? Kringström's orchestra is supposed to be pretty good."

Joel went stiff.

Why could he never learn not to keep shooting off his mouth? Just think if Samuel got it into his head to take Sara to the dance at the Community Center on Saturday night?

"Kringström's orchestra is pretty awful," he said.

"Have you heard them?" asked Samuel in surprise.

"Everybody says so," said Joel. "They are the worst orchestra in Sweden."

"I've heard the opposite," said Samuel. "Maybe I should go and hear them, and see who's right?"

"You'll regret it if you do," Joel insisted.

Samuel put down his newspaper and eyed him intently.

"You seem to know an awful lot about Kringström's orchestra," he said. "But isn't it a bit early for you to start thinking about going out dancing?"

He ruffled Joel's hair, and returned to his newspaper.

Joel went to his room and breathed a sigh of relief.

That was a close shave, he thought. Geronimo Gustafson's big plan had very nearly collapsed in ruins. Samuel came close to making up his mind to take Sara to the dance at the Community Center.

Now Geronimo could breathe a sigh of relief. There was nothing in the way any longer.

But he was wrong, Joel Geronimo Gustafson. When

Saturday came round and Samuel had made porridge and they were having breakfast together, he suddenly put down his spoon and looked at Joel and said:

"That was a very good suggestion you came up with."

Joel didn't know what his dad was talking about. He hadn't made any suggestions, as far as he knew.

"Sara and I are going to shake a leg at the Community Center tonight," said Samuel.

Joel couldn't believe his ears.

But it was true. And in a strange way, it was Joel who had set it up.

He stared down at his porridge in the same way as he'd stared down at his desktop a few days before.

What was he going to do now?

Would he never be able to do his good deed? Was he going to have to drag this Miracle around like a millstone for the rest of his life?

When he finished eating he went to his room. Samuel was doing the washing-up, humming away all the time.

How was Joel going to solve this problem?

What was he going to do now?

Geronimo Gustafson. What on earth were you going to do now?

— TEN —

General Custer, Joel thought.

Or Geronimo. Or both of them together. They wouldn't have coped with this. Not even together!

Once it had dawned on him that Samuel and Sara really had made up their minds to go dancing to Kringström's orchestra that night, Joel felt that all was lost. The good deed he had spent so much time and effort organizing and was on the point of achieving would never happen now.

He was back where he'd started. Just like when he took a wrong turning in Simon Windstorm's maze. The good deed was something he'd never be able to find his way out of. He'd have to keep pressing on with attempts to do a good deed until he was so old that he couldn't even stand up anymore.

He sat in his room, swearing. He muttered all the swearwords he could think of. And he invented several new ones. All the time, Samuel was bustling around in the kitchen, humming tunes. He filled the big zinc bathtub with hot water. Then he shouted for Joel to come and scrub his back for him. Joel would have preferred to hit Samuel on the head with the brush instead. Why did Samuel have to choose tonight of all nights to go out dancing with Sara? Why not next Saturday? Why not every Saturday apart from this one?

Why couldn't grown-ups ever understand when it wasn't acceptable for them to go out dancing?

Joel scrubbed and Samuel grunted. If the brush had been impregnated with a sleeping potion, Samuel would have fallen asleep on the spot and not woken up until tomorrow. Joel would pay Kringström and his orchestra and he would rent the whole of the Community Center for tomorrow night so that Sara and Samuel could dance together then. But not tonight! Alas, the brush was not poisoned and Samuel continued humming. He stood in the middle of the floor in a pool of water, shaving.

"We'll have dinner together at Sara's place this evening," he said contentedly. "Then we'll go dancing. You can stay in her flat and listen to the radio if you like."

"No," said Joel.

"Why not?" wondered Samuel. "Sara's a very good cook. Much better than you and me."

"I don't want to," said Joel.

160

Samuel grew angry. Or perhaps irritated. Joel wasn't quite sure of the difference.

"Just this once you'll do as I say!" said Samuel.

"No," said Joel and emptied the bathtub by pouring bucket after bucket of dirty water down the sink.

"What are you going to eat, then?" asked Samuel.

I shall starve, Joel thought.

But he didn't say that, of course.

"I'll make my own dinner," he said instead. "You said I was good at looking after myself. You did say that, didn't you?"

"Perhaps I did," said Samuel. "I just don't understand why you're making yourself so difficult to get along with."

Joel said nothing.

Neither did Samuel.

Another kind of silence, Joel thought. Different from the one in the forest or in the Underworld.

At six o'clock Joel knotted Samuel's tie for him.

"Are you sure you don't want to come?" Samuel asked again.

"I prefer to stay at home," said Joel.

"Please yourself, then," said Samuel, and left. Joel didn't bother to stand in the window and wave. He went straight to his room. He lay down on his bed and pulled the covers over his head. An hour and a half from now he was due at the back door of the Community Center. That's what had been arranged. But it would be impossible now.

He sat straight up in bed.

"Oh, hell!" he yelled at nobody in particular. Then he lay down again with the covers over his head.

Why does everything go wrong? he wondered. You do the right thing. But it goes wrong even so.

Why is life so difficult?

He got out of bed. Lying there with the covers over his head didn't help. He checked the kitchen clock. Seventeen minutes past six. The clock didn't have a second hand, so he tried to count sixty seconds. But the clock showed eighteen minutes past six when he'd only got as far as forty-nine. He was counting too slowly.

I give up, he thought. The Caviar Man and Gertrud will have to manage without me. If there is a God, he'll have to do without a thank-you for his Miracle. He can send the police after me for all I care. I, Joel Gustafson, couldn't care less about that.

But at that very moment, he had an idea. He would disguise himself. Surely he could dress up so that nobody would recognize him? He'd be able to hide behind the fat drummer, Holmström. He was the fattest man in town. The fattest drummer in the world.

He looked at the clock again. Twenty-four minutes past six. He cursed for not having made up his mind sooner.

Joella, he thought. I can dress up as a girl. I can tell Kringström that unfortunately my brother is ill, but I'd also like to learn to play the saxophone. . . .

No, that's not possible, he thought immediately. I can't wear Mummy Jenny's dress. And there isn't anything else.

He checked the clock again. Nearly half past six.

When ten past seven came round, he still hadn't thought of a good way of disguising himself. He would have to go now. Yet again he'd decided to stay at home, but the moment he'd pulled the covers over his head, he'd bounced back up again. He would have to go! He took Samuel's hat from the wardrobe, the one he'd bought in Hull. He pulled it down over his eyes. Then he took Samuel's spare pair of reading glasses and let them hang down over his nose. That was all. He raced down the stairs and out into the chilly evening air. It will soon be winter, he thought. It will snow before long.

He ran so fast that he got a stitch. He had to pause and catch his breath. Then he set off running again. As the church clock chimed twice, he arrived at the Community Center. Kringström's big Ford was backed into the courtyard. The members of the orchestra were already busy unloading their instruments. The fattest drummer in the world was carrying the big bass drum in front of him, looking as if he had an extra stomach. The double bass player was perched on the car roof, untying the rope round his instrument case. Joel knew that his name was Ross—but was that his first name or his surname? Just then Kringström came out the back door with the Community Center manager, Mr. Engman. Joel stopped dead when he heard that they were quarreling.

"Of course we have to have a bulb that works in our

dressing room," growled Kringström. "Do you expect us to get changed in the pitch black? Are we supposed to drink our coffee in darkness during the interval?"

"You don't drink coffee," said Engman testily. "You drink vodka and whisky. And then you are all so drunk, you can hardly hold your instruments."

"Take that back here and now," roared Kringström. "If not, you can find yourself another orchestra."

The quarrel ended as quickly as it had begun. Engman vanished through the back door, muttering away to himself.

Joel stepped forward.

Kringström looked at him in surprise.

"What's all this?" he asked. "A dwarf in a hat?"

"I'm the one who wants to learn to play the saxophone," said Joel, raising his hat. Kringström burst out laughing. He explained to the other members of the orchestra who Joel was. As if Joel had been a grown-up, they all marched up to shake him by the hand. Ross's first name was Einar. The world's fattest drummer had a hand so big that Joel's disappeared inside it.

"We'd better get a move on!" shouted Kringström. "The pack of wolves will be after us before we know where we are."

Joel helped to carry the instruments.

"What pack of wolves?" he asked Ross.

"The audience," said Ross. "The audience is a pack of wolves. If we don't play well, they gobble us up."

It didn't take long to unpack the instruments. The sheet music was distributed and placed in the correct order, and they started tuning up. Each of them would occasionally take a swig from a bottle that was passed round from hand to hand. The manager, Engman, appeared and assured the orchestra that he had replaced the broken lightbulb.

"So, we'd better get changed," said Kringström to Joel. "Stay here on the stage and keep an eye on the instruments."

Joel was alone onstage. The empty auditorium in front of him was suddenly full of people. Everybody was waiting for Joel Gustafson's Orchestra to start playing. Joel did what he'd heard you were supposed to do. He stamped on the floor, beating time, counted to four and raised his saxophone.

Kringström was in the wings, tying his bow tie. He noticed Joel's solo performance, and signaled to the other members of the orchestra. They stood in the wings and watched Joel. Then they all ran onto the stage and started playing pretend instruments as well. When Joel realized what was happening, he stopped playing. But Kringström urged him on.

Another kind of silence, Joel thought. The silent instruments' orchestra . . .

Kringström took over.

"We'd better stop now if we're going to have time to change before the pack of wolves closes in on us."

"That sounded great," said the World's Fattest Drummer, patting Joel on the shoulder with his gigantic hand.

Joel blushed. It was only a game, after all! A game that somebody who'd soon be twelve was too old for...

Then he felt his worries creeping up on him again. No game in the whole world could change reality. That's what it was, full stop. Soon Sara and Samuel would appear. And Gertrud and the Caviar Man. And the pack of wolves.

He looked at the big curtain hanging behind the orchestra. It was like an enormous painting—even bigger than the altarpiece in the church. It was summer on the curtain. A blue lake was glistening. Birch trees had come into leaf. Blue and green. There was a white seagull soaring up in the sky. Joel went behind the curtain. It was dark and dusty there. But what he had done was to exit from the autumn of the world outside this stage, and to enter into summer instead. That was the way it should always be. You should live in a house in which every room was a different season. So that you could choose. The kitchen could be summer and the bedroom spring. The pantry could be winter and the hall autumn....

He discovered that there was a peephole in the tall curtain. He could stand behind one of the white birch trees and look out into the auditorium. People had started to come in. Girls with their hair up and in high heels. Boys in black winkle-pickers with Brylcreemed hair. Joel could see that there was a logjam at the very back of the room. Mr. Engman, the manager, was waving his arms about. Suddenly everything turned black before Joel's eyes. It was Ross walking over the stage and starting to tune his double bass. More and more people were entering the auditorium. The light was dimmed. But there was a hell of a noise already. The girls were standing in clusters by one of the walls. Joel knew it was called the Mountain Wall. The boys were gathered by the opposite wall. Somebody kicked the floor, as if he were a horse. Somebody slapped somebody else on the back. More and more people were turning up. But not Sara and Samuel. And not the Caviar Man nor Gertrud either.

Now the orchestra was in place. A row of footlights shone red and yellow. Joel was standing behind the curtain, but was almost blinded. All the members of the orchestra were wearing red jackets now. Kringström's face was already sweaty.

Then they started playing. Not many people danced at first. Some of the boys ventured over to the Mountain Wall, but they soon retreated to the opposite wall again. All the time Joel was keeping an eye on the swing doors, where Engman was trying to keep the Pack of Wolves under control. None of those Joel was expecting to see had arrived as yet. But it was starting to get crowded out there now. Queues were forming at the swing doors. Engman was flailing his arms about. The orchestra started to play another tune. It was a faster beat. More people were dancing now. A group of boys were standing in front of the stage, watching the orchestra. They were not dancing. They were just watching and listening.

Then Joel noticed Sara and Samuel. Engman was still flailing his arms about, and Sara and Samuel made their way through the throng.

They can't see me here, Joel thought. Not while I'm hidden behind this birch tree.

Now they were dancing. Samuel had his arm round Sara. It looked as if he were jumping. He was sticking his bottom out and pushing Sara along in front of him. Joel started laughing behind his birch tree. He'd never seen Samuel like that before. His eyes were glued to Sara and Samuel, and he forgot all about keeping an eye on the swing doors. Only when the dance had finished and Sara was wiping the sweat from her face did he remember that he had to keep a check on who came in. It was as crowded as ever around the doors. He couldn't see either the Caviar Man or Gertrud.

It's Samuel's fault, he thought in annoyance. If he hadn't brought Sara here, I'd never have forgotten to keep an eye on the swing doors.

The orchestra started playing again. Sara and Samuel were dancing. Joel kept his eyes peeled. He suddenly caught sight of the Caviar Man. He could see the back of his head among all the couples on the dance floor. But then he realized it wasn't the Caviar Man after all. It was somebody else. And where was Gertrud?

168

They're not going to turn up, he thought. It's gone wrong again. . . .

It was hard work, peering through the hole in the birch tree. He had to lean forward all the time in order to see. When the orchestra finished playing, he stood erect and stretched. He walked to the edge of the birch woods and looked out into the auditorium. The World's Fattest Drummer was wiping the sweat from his brow. Kringström put down his saxophone and picked up the clarinet instead.

"Siam Blues," Kringström shouted. "Are you ready?"

He stamped his foot to beat the rhythm, and Joel did the same. Just as Kringström played the first note, Joel saw the Caviar Man.

He was in the group gathered in front of the stage, watching the orchestra.

Joel dodged quickly back into the shadowy wings. Were his eyes deceiving him again? No, it was the Caviar Man, all right. He'd come!

The Caviar Man seemed to be staring up wistfully at the orchestra. His lips kept moving, as if he were playing an invisible saxophone. Just like Joel. He suddenly turned round and looked behind him. He's looking for Gertrud, Joel thought. But it wasn't Gertrud who'd poked him in the back. It was somebody else. The Caviar Man looked angry. He tried to make himself a bit more room.

Then it all turned pitch-black in front of Joel. It was the World's Fattest Drummer who'd moved his stool slightly and landed slap bang in front of the peephole. Joel couldn't see a thing. He went back to the wings. It wasn't such a good place as behind the curtain—if the Caviar Man suddenly turned his head, he'd be able to see Joel watching him. The same applied to all the couples who were dancing. They could see him as well. Now he had to look in several directions all at once. I could do with some extra eyes, he thought. At least another ten...

When the orchestra took a rest and left the stage, Joel started to get worried. Why hasn't Gertrud come? he wondered. Surely she must have been pleased to receive another letter from the Caviar Man.

"What do you think you're doing here?" said a voice behind him.

Joel was so startled, he almost jumped out of the wings and onto the stage.

It was the Community Center manager, Engman. He looked angry.

"What's a little kid like you doing in here?" he said, looking even more angry. "This is for grown-ups. How did you get in?"

Nothing annoyed Engman more that people trying to sneak into a dance or a film show. Joel had heard lots of stories about what Engman could do when he was angry.

"I belong to the orchestra," he said, his voice shaking.

Engman stared at him.

"Are you Kringström's lad?" he asked.

"Yes," said Joel. "He's my dad."

"OK," said Engman. "In that case you can stay here."

Engman disappeared into the wings. What will happen if he starts talking to Kringström, Joel wondered. But he calmed down when he realized that they talk to each other as little as possible. They were not exactly the best of friends.

The Caviar Man had vanished. It was completely empty in front of the stage. Joel leaned forward cautiously and looked out into the big dance hall. He could see a crowd of people at the doors leading into the café, but there was no sign of the Caviar Man. Nor could he see Samuel and Sara. He made up his mind to recapture his peephole behind the birch tree. If he could move the stool behind the drums slightly, the World's Fattest Drummer wouldn't be sitting in the way anymore. All the musicians were in the changing room. He peered out into the hall again. There were a few people out there, but nobody was looking at the stage. He leapt like a tiger towards the drummer's stool, but needless to say, he bumped into a music stand. When he thrusted an arm out to maintain his balance, he accidentally punched one of the cymbals. The sound echoed around the hall. He lost his hat and his glasses and tumbled down among the drums. He recovered the hat straightaway, but the glasses must have landed under the big bass drum. He wedged his hand beneath the drum and retrieved them, then raced back into the wings again. He looked across at the wings on the other side of the stage, and saw the World's Fattest

Drummer staring anxiously at his drums. Joel sidled back into the shadows. The big man on the other side of the stage shrugged, and went away. Joel could breathe again. He moved back to his place in the wings where he could see into the auditorium.

Sara was standing in the middle of the dance floor, looking at him. Straight at him.

He'd been rumbled! Joel realized that there was no point dodging back into the shadows. Sara had discovered him. She must have been somewhere out there, heard the noise when he hit the cymbal and recognized him.

But where was Samuel? Had Samuel rumbled him as well? Joel looked at Sara. She stared back at him, as if she couldn't believe her eyes. Then she broke into a smile. Smiled and shook her head. At the same time Joel noticed Samuel. He was coming out of the door to the café.

Joel raised a finger to his lips. Would Sara understand?

Yes, she understood. She nodded and raised her own index finger to her lips.

Joel took a step back. Now he couldn't be seen. But he could hear Samuel's voice.

"What are you staring at?" Samuel asked.

"I think there was a cat in the wings over there," said Sara.

"A cat?" said Samuel in surprise.

"I may have been mistaken," said Sara. "It was probably nothing."

Joel stood motionless in the shadows. It was a big

moment when you fell in love with somebody. Now Joel was in love with Sara. She hadn't said anything. She'd turned Joel into a cat. He knew she would keep his secret.

She must wonder, Joel thought. He made up his mind to tell her why he'd gone to the Community Center. He'd tell her one of these days. Sometime in the future . . .

The orchestra returned to the stage and the buzz of chatter increased in the hall. Joel peered at the wall where the girls had gathered in little groups. Still no sign of Gertrud. But the Caviar Man had reappeared. He was standing with a group of other young men in front of the stage. They were in a circle with their heads down. Joel could see that they were looking at something, but no matter how hard he tried, he couldn't make out what it was.

Kringström started stamping his foot again, the red and yellow lights were switched on and he raised his saxophone to his mouth. But the group of young men in front of the stage had their backs turned on the orchestra. They were laughing at whatever it was they were looking at. The saxophone was playing, but the young men were laughing. The Caviar Man was laughing louder than anybody else.

Then Joel realized what it was they were laughing at.

The Caviar Man was holding a sheet of paper. A sheet of paper that Joel recognized.

It was the letter from Gertrud. The letter Joel had written himself. On his dad's writing paper.

Joel went all stiff. The Caviar Man was showing his

mates the letter from Gertrud, the letter that Joel had written. He was showing the secret letter to his friends. And they were all laughing. They were laughing so loudly that you could hardly hear the saxophone.

Only a couple of minutes before, he had started to love somebody. Sara.

Now he was starting to hate the Caviar Man. And when Joel saw that they had stopped laughing, and the Caviar Man had torn the letter into little pieces and dropped them on the floor, where a thousand heels would grind them into the dust, Joel hated the man more than he had ever hated any other person before. It was as if the Caviar Man had trampled on Gertrud. . . .

Joel walked away. He went down the stairs leading to the back door where they had carried in the instruments. He unlocked it and went out. It was autumn now. Cold, with a sky full of stars. You could hardly hear the saxophone anymore. But the Caviar Man's laughter was still echoing inside his head.

It was noisy in front of the Community Center. All the people Engman had refused to allow in were gathered there. Somebody was holding on to a drainpipe and throwing up. A portable gramophone was blaring out from a passing car.

Then Joel saw Gertrud.

She was standing in the shadows on the other side of the street. Staring up at the illuminated entrance.

Don't go in, Joel thought. Go home. The Caviar Man is not worth having. I was wrong....

Gertrud took a pace forward. She was now in the light from a lamppost. Joel could see that she was wearing her best overcoat. The one she had made herself from curtains and dresses, with fox fur trim. Where her nose ought to have been she had her best handkerchief, the one made of Chinese silk.

She set off over the road towards the entrance. Joel ran over to her. He stopped in front of her, in the middle of the street.

"Joel!" she said in surprise. "What a funny hat you're wearing!"

"Don't go in there," said Joel. "Don't do it."

"I feel like dancing," she said.

"Don't go in there," Joel said again.

She stared at him in astonishment.

"What's the matter with you?" she asked. "I have to meet somebody in there."

"I know," said Joel. "Don't go."

Gertrud couldn't understand what was going on. What did he mean? And why was he dressed up? Wearing a strange hat and glasses?

Now she turned serious. Her voice was sharp. As sharp as a knife, Joel thought. She's going to cut me open.

"What do you know?" she asked. She was speaking so loudly that some of the young people loitering nearby had started to show an interest, and listened to what was going on.

"What do you know?" She was almost bellowing now. "WHAT DO YOU KNOW?"

"It was me who wrote those letters!" Joel shouted. "I didn't mean any harm!"

Gertrud looked at him. Her eyes were like ice.

"I didn't mean any harm," said Joel again. "I thought you and the Caviar Man could get married."

"The Caviar Man?" she exclaimed. "What are you talking about?"

She grabbed hold of him. Gave him a good shaking. Curious onlookers gathered round. Formed a circle round them. A car that couldn't get past sounded its horn angrily.

"What are you talking about?" she bellowed again.

"It was me who wrote those letters!" yelled Joel.

She eyed him up and down. The penny dropped.

Then she boxed his ears. His hat and glasses fell off and danced around on the cobblestones. She hit Joel so hard that his head was buzzing. He almost fell over. As if through a fog, he saw Gertrud running away. Her coat was fluttering like a bird with a broken wing. All around him people were laughing and giggling.

"What's going on here?" somebody asked.

"Noseless Gertrud has been fighting," somebody answered.

Joel wished there were a manhole cover in front of his

feet. So that he could lift it up and disappear into the Underworld. Perhaps there was a passage down there that led to the sea? Or a tunnel that ran to where Mummy Jenny was?

He picked up the hat and glasses, and ran away.

Behind him, he could hear people laughing.

Gertrud had vanished.

His cheeks were burning. Now I'm on fire, Joel thought. That dream has come true. I've started to burn. Before long there'll be flames coming from my cheeks.

He kept on running all the way home. When he got there he felt as if he were going to be sick.

Life had suddenly become so hard.

There were too many questions.

Maybe that's what distinguishes children from grown-ups, he thought.

Understanding that there are so many questions that don't have answers?

He trudged slowly up the stairs.

All the time, in his mind's eye, he could see Gertrud in front of him.

Her coat flapping like the broken wing of a bird.

You can get lost inside yourself, Joel thought.

You don't have to go into the forest in order to get lost.

You have Day and Night inside yourself. And when twilight falls inside you, the shadows become so long....

— ELEVEN —

Joel couldn't hide his misery.

Needless to say, Samuel realized immediately that there was something wrong.

That was also the fault of Eklund and the Ljusdal bus. Before the accident, Samuel had been like all other grown-ups. Easily fooled. If Joel didn't want to tell his dad that he wasn't feeling very well, or that he hadn't been to school, Samuel never noticed a thing. And as he didn't notice anything, he didn't ask any questions. But that was before the accident. Now Samuel seemed to look at Joel in a different way. Not a day went by without Samuel asking Joel how he was. It had become more difficult to fool Samuel.

Joel was awake when Samuel got back home. It had turned midnight.

"Are you still awake?" Samuel asked. "Why aren't you asleep?"

"I don't know," said Joel. "But I'm going to put the light out now."

"I can tell you that dancing was great fun," said Samuel. "That was a terrific idea you came up with."

Samuel switched off the light and left. Joel had a bit of a stomachache. His face no longer hurt from the slap Gertrud had given him. The pain had crept down into his stomach. But it wasn't the usual stomachache. It felt as if there were fingers inside there, scratching him.

Joel had felt the same kind of pain once before. It was when he thought Samuel had abandoned him, and vanished in the same way as his Mummy Jenny. On that occasion, Joel had thrown a stone through Sara's window.

If only he could have told Samuel what had happened! The whole complicated story that had begun when Joel had been careless and fallen under the Ljusdal bus. The good deed he'd tried to carry out, but everything had gone wrong.

But he couldn't tell Samuel about it. His dad wouldn't understand a thing. And he might well become very angry.

The next morning Joel woke up very early. He'd had a nightmare. When he opened his eyes in the darkness, he couldn't remember what he'd dreamt. Perhaps he'd been on fire again? He looked at the alarm clock on a stool beside his bed: a quarter past six. As it was Sunday, he didn't need to get up. He could stay in his warm bed all day if he wanted to. He could hear Samuel snoring on the other side of the dividing wall.

There was a crunching noise in the wall next to his ear. A wood mouse was busy gnawing away at something or other. Joel tried to go back to sleep. He closed his eyes, and now he was out in the forest again. He still hadn't found that secret tree. But he knew now that it was very close by. A squirrel was sitting on a branch, looking at him. There was something odd about that squirrel. And then Joel realized that it was in fact a monkey....

He opened his eyes again. He couldn't concentrate on looking for that secret tree. All of a sudden Gertrud appeared, in the middle of his story, and gave him a box on the ear.

Joel got up and dressed. Then he went to the kitchen and drank a glass of milk. It would soon start getting light. Then he could go out. He enjoyed cycling around town on a Sunday morning. There was never anybody about. He could imagine that he was the only individual still alive. He was the ruler of the Wasteland....

It was chilly outside. The saddle was wet. He could hear Simon Windstorm's lorry in the distance. So it's started again, he thought. Simon can't get to sleep at night. The sound of the lorry annoyed Joel. He didn't want to see Simon Windstorm just now. He wanted to be left in peace.

He wondered why it was so easy to think when he was on his bike. What did the wheels have to do with his head? Were they a sort of dynamo that set his thoughts in motion?

He hissed at himself.

Why did he have so many silly thoughts? Had he inherited that from his mother, Jenny? If so, perhaps it was just as well that she had run away?

He stopped outside the bar and dismounted. The CLOSED notice was displayed. The bar didn't open until one o'clock on a Sunday. But the beery locals used to gather outside at about twelve. They often had bottles of the hard stuff in their inside pockets that they used to share before Ludde removed the CLOSED notice and unlocked the door.

Maybe it would have been better if a Miracle hadn't happened, he thought dejectedly. Then at least I wouldn't have been slapped by Gertrud.

He remounted his bike and started pedalling as fast as he could. He was being chased by a terrifying gang of murderers. He could feel them panting on the back of his neck. Faster! He had to go faster, faster. . . .

He had a puncture outside the post office. There was a swishing noise, and his front tire went flat. When he examined the wheel, he saw that a nail had got stuck in the tire. A big rusty nail.

I'll get rid of this damned bike, he thought. He was furious.

I'll wheel it as far as the bridge and throw it into the river.

Then he heard somebody shouting. He looked round. There was nobody there. Then there came another shout. Somebody was waving to him from an upstairs window over the post office. That was where the Swedish Telegraph Office was. Joel could see that it was Asta. Asta Bagge was the local manager for Swedish Telegraph. Was she shouting at him? He wheeled his bike over the street. Asta had fiery red hair, and was so thin you had to suspect that she ran herself through the mangle every morning after getting up. Joel didn't know anybody as flat as Asta Bagge.

"Can you do me a favor?" she shouted to him.

"Of course," Joel said.

"Go round to the back," Asta shouted. "And up the stairs. The door's not locked."

Joel leaned his bike against the wall and went round the corner. He'd never been in the Telegraph premises before. When he opened the door and went in, Asta was sitting in front of the big telephone exchange, and connecting a long-distance call.

"Go ahead, Karlskrona," she said into the microphone hanging in front of her face. Then she flicked a little black switch, and stood up.

"It's a good job I saw you," she said. "What's your name?"

"Joel Gustafson," said Joel.

"Now you can do me a favor," said Asta. "I'll give you a little reward for your trouble. Do you know where I live?"

"No," said Joel.

"There's a house behind the bakery," said Asta. "A red one."

Joel knew the one she was talking about.

"I think I forgot to switch off the cooker when I came to work," said Asta. "Take these keys and hurry over to my flat and check for me, please. Don't forget to lock up again when you leave."

Joel hurried off. Now he was the only one who could stop the raging prairie fire from spreading to the pioneers' camp. They would lose everything if he didn't get there in time. . . .

He unlocked the door and went into Asta's flat. There was a smell of perfume. Perfume and honey. He wiped his feet and looked round for the kitchen. He noticed the corner of a draining board through a door standing ajar. He opened the door wide. The cooker certainly was on. One of the hot plates was red hot. He switched it off. Then he explored the little flat. There was a smell of perfume everywhere. Joel imagined that he was a burglar. He was looking for money that was hidden somewhere, but he didn't know where. And jewelry. He avoided touching anything, so as not to leave any fingerprints. A row of photographs in brown frames was lined up on a bureau. Children stared at him, wide-eyed. An old man was sitting on a bench by a house wall. A poodle was wagging its tail. Joel opened the door to Asta's bedroom. The bed was unmade. The smell of perfume was even stronger inside there.

There was something odd about the flat, but Joel couldn't put his finger on it. He looked round. Now he was the detective, searching for clues that the burglar had left behind. He suspected the culprit might be the notorious Joel Gustafson. The master thief who had never been caught.

Then he realized what was odd about the flat. There was no telephone. Asta was in charge of the Telegraph Office, but she didn't have a telephone of her own! It was a mystery. He went through the rooms one more time. The hot plate was no longer red. There was no sign of a telephone anywhere.

He took another look at the photograph of the poodle. Then he left, locking the door carefully behind him.

He checked three times, to make sure.

When he got back to the Telegraph Office, Asta was sitting at the switchboard knitting. The earphones were hanging round her neck.

"The cooker was on, in fact," Joel said.

"How awful!" said Asta. "That's never happened before. The place could have burnt down."

She opened her purse and took out two one-krona coins. Two kronor just for switching off a cooker? Joel bowed politely when she gave him the money. Perhaps that was a job he could have when he grew up? A cooker-turner-offer? If he got two kronor every time, he'd soon be so rich that he'd be able to buy the Pontiac in Krage's showroom.

Joel stared curiously at the big telephone exchange. Somebody rang again, and Asta connected the call. He asked and she explained how it worked. Joel soon thought he'd be able to connect calls himself.

Things quieted down again, and Asta took off the earphones.

"Is the exchange open at night as well?" Joel asked.

"It's always open," said Asta. "I'll have the night shift next week. There are three of us who take it in turns. We have a bed in the back room over there, where we can sleep. But somebody always has to be here in case a call comes through. It could be an emergency. Somebody might be ill. Somebody might be about to give birth and need a taxi."

There was another ring. Asta answered, and connected the caller to the number requested. Then came three more calls at the same time. Asta connected them. Somebody wanted to speak to Stockholm. Asta connected. And connected. And connected.

Joel saw a local telephone directory lying on a table. He leafed through it. He came to the letter *L*. Then he saw the name Lundberg, David. Telephone number 135.

The Caviar Man had a telephone!

Joel dropped the directory as if it had burnt his fingers.

Asta hadn't noticed anything. "You're through to Stockholm," she said into the microphone.

"Do many people ring during the night?" Joel asked when she had removed the earphones again.

"Hardly anybody rings after midnight," she said, picking up her knitting again. Joel could see that it was going to be a child's sweater.

"I'd better be going now," said Joel.

"Thank you for your help," said Asta. Then it rang again.

Joel wheeled his bike home. He had a repair kit in the cellar, and would be able to mend the tire. But it wasn't the bicycle he was thinking about as he walked. The Caviar Man had a telephone! That damned numbskull who had spied on Gertrud and then cursed and sneaked away. Slunk away like a cowardly dog.

Joel had decided that it was all the Caviar Man's fault.

He stopped dead.

He would get his revenge on the Caviar Man. That would be the good deed he would do so that he needn't worry about the Miracle anymore. He would get his revenge on the Caviar Man for having spied on Gertrud and sworn at her. It would be a good deed—nobody would know that Joel had done it. But perhaps that didn't matter? Surely the main thing was that the good deed had been carried out? Surely a good deed could be as invisible as God? After all, everybody talked about God, but nobody had seen him, had they?

Joel started walking again.

He was thinking about Asta and her telephone exchange.

By the time he got home and opened the gate, he'd made up his mind. He knew now how he was going to get his revenge on the Caviar Man. Then Gertrud would understand that he had meant well when he wrote those secret letters. Everything would return to normal.

Two days later, on Tuesday, Samuel went away. He was going elk hunting and would be away for two days and nights. He had suggested that Joel should live at Sara's place while he was away, but Joel had objected. He could look after himself. Samuel had eventually given way. Joel had promised to have dinner with Sara those two evenings.

"But what will you do if you have nightmares?" Samuel had asked.

"Then I'll go round to Sara's," said Joel.

"You're a clever lad," he said. "I've never really thought about it before, but the fact is, you can manage on your own as well as a grown-up."

Joel felt proud.

As well as a grown-up, Samuel had said.

Perhaps that's what happens when you're forced to be your own mother?

On Tuesday afternoon Samuel came home from the forest earlier than usual. He'd already packed his rucksack that morning. The big rifle was lying in its case on the kitchen bench. It seemed to Joel that Samuel was acting like a child on Christmas Eve. Could it really be that much fun, standing in the freezing-cold forest and hoping that an elk would come lumbering past? Samuel went elk hunting every year. He always returned home without having shot an elk. He hadn't even seen one. It was always somebody else in the hunting party who'd shot the beast.

A horn sounded in the street below.

"Are you sure you'll be able to manage?" Samuel asked.

"Of course," said Joel. "Off you go now! Go and shoot an elk!"

When he reached the street Samuel turned round and waved to Joel, who was standing in the window. Then he clambered into the waiting car, and they set off.

Joel had thought out his plan in detail. He'd packed a rucksack and hidden it under his bed. When it was time to go to Sara's, he put on his boots and jacket, and set off. It had become a bit warmer. But it was drizzling.

Sara had made meatballs. Joel thought it was important that he didn't eat too much. If he did, it would make him tired. The meatballs were lovely, but he forced himself not to eat too many.

"Didn't you like them?" asked Sara, looking disappointed.

"Yes, they were very good," said Joel. "But I've eaten so many."

It was ice cream for afters. He found it hard not to eat too much.

Sara was still looking worried.

"Don't you feel well?" she asked.

"I'm just a bit tired," said Joel. "I'll go home and go to bed early tonight."

"Are you sure you don't want to sleep here?" Sara asked.

"I always sleep best in my own bed," said Joel.

"You're a remarkable little man," said Sara, shaking her head. "Anybody would think you were a grown-up already."

Joel was back home by eight o'clock. He went into Samuel's room and fetched a blanket. Then he lay down on top of his bed with the blanket over him. He'd set the alarm clock for midnight. He'd moved the stool farther away, so that he'd be forced to get out of bed in order to switch off the alarm when it rang. He tossed and turned for ages before falling asleep.

He woke up with a start when the alarm went off. His head was buzzing, and he couldn't remember why he'd woken up. Then it dawned on him. He was wide awake in a flash. To build up his strength before his nocturnal expedition, he went to the pantry and ate a few spoonfuls of jam. Then he crept cautiously down the stairs and out into the street.

The sky was covered by heavy clouds. It was raining.

He hurried towards the Telegraph Office. Then he heard Simon Windstorm's lorry approaching. He managed to hide himself in the shadows until it had gone past. Once this was all over, he'd pay another visit to Simon. Once he'd done his good deed and could forget all about ever having been involved in a Miracle...

The lights were on in the Telegraph Office windows. He crept along in the shadows to the back of the building and made his way to the door. It wasn't locked. He walked slowly up the stairs, counting them as he went. When he came to the ninth step he paused and heaved himself up onto the twelfth with the help of the banister rail. He'd noticed the first time he'd walked up those stairs that the tenth and eleventh steps creaked. He listened in the darkness outside the door. A faint strip of light shone onto the landing through the crack underneath the door. He peeped in through the keyhole. The chair in front of the telephone exchange was empty. He turned the handle ever so carefully and opened the door. He could hear snores coming from the back room. He closed the door and carefully took off his rucksack. Then he tiptoed to the door of the back room. Asta Bagge was lying on top of the bed, asleep. The blue jumper she'd been knitting had fallen on the floor. Joel closed the door. Then he hurried over to the switchboard. Yes, he could remember what to do. But he wasn't going to receive any incoming calls. He was going to make some calls himself.

He recited in his head what he needed to do. Plug a cable into the number he wanted to call, turn on the switch that would make the telephone ring in the house of whoever he wanted to speak to, keep the microphone switched on and speak when the person at the other end had lifted the receiver.

But it would be some time before he could make his first call. He had a lot to do before he was ready. He took his logbook and a pencil from his pocket. Then he fetched the telephone directory. He started working his way through all the names, in alphabetical order. Now and then he noted down a number on the inside cover of his logbook. It was the only place where there was any space left.

When he'd got as far as the letter *F*, there was a buzzing noise from the exchange. He'd been expecting that. Even so, he thought he reacted much too slowly. He closed the telephone directory, took his logbook and pencil, and hid behind a cupboard. No sooner had he ducked down behind the cupboard than Asta Bagge came shuffling out of the room where she'd been asleep.

Then he saw the rucksack.

He'd forgotten it. It was next to the entrance door.

Numbskull, he thought. Numbskull, numbskull . . .

Asta had sat down in front of the telephone exchange and put on her earphones. Joel knew that he would have to retrieve the rucksack now. She couldn't avoid seeing it when she returned to the back room.

Asta responded to the call.

Joel tiptoed over the floor, grabbed his rucksack and dashed back to his haven behind the cupboard.

"What's all this nonsense?" said Asta Bagge.

Joel thought he'd been rumbled. He was in a right mess now.

But then it dawned on him that Asta was angry with the person who'd made the call.

"The telephone is not a little boy's toy," said Asta Bagge, and sounded really angry. "You are drunk, and should go and lie down and go to sleep instead of ringing here and talking nonsense. Good night!"

Asta switched off and went back to bed.

Joel waited until he heard her snoring again.

Then he went back and continued sorting through the telephone directory. By the time he'd finished he had twelve numbers. Before starting on his mission, he felt he needed to take a breather behind the cupboard. He'd packed a few jam sandwiches in his rucksack. He ate two of them before he felt up to starting off on what he planned to do.

Asta was snoring. Spluttering and wheezing. Joel sat down in front of the switchboard. He had the numbers listed in front of him. He started making the various connections. There was the Reverend Nyblom's number. Then Mr. Malm, the chief of police. Lieutenant Colonel Ceder, and the headmaster, Mr. Gottfried. Local newspaper editor Mr. Waltin... Twelve numbers in all. He made all the relevant connections. He could feel his heart beating, and he was covered in sweat. He slowly moved his right hand towards the switch that would start all the telephone numbers ringing at the same time.

The Lord of the Night, Joel thought. I'm going to wake the whole lot of you up now.

He threw the switch, and stared expectantly at the maze of connections on the exchange in front of him. When somebody answered, a lamp would start blinking. He adjusted a switch in order to make sure that the ringing wouldn't be heard at the exchange.

Why didn't anybody answer? Had he made a mistake? Come on now, answer. Answer. . . .

Now the first light started flashing. It was Lieutenant Colonel Ceder. Then Mr. Waltin's number started winking, the newspaper editor. Before long the whole switchboard was covered in flashing lights. Joel pressed the button and started talking into the microphone. He grunted and growled in order to make sure that nobody would recognize his voice, and tried to keep the volume down so that Asta Bagge wouldn't wake up.

"The Caviar Man is a scoundrel," he hissed. "He spies on innocent people. He hides in the shadows. All shadows grow in the twilight. I repeat. The Caviar Man is a scoundrel. His shadow is long when twilight falls."

Joel repeated his message over and over again. He could hear the indignant, sleepy, surprised voices wondering who was ringing, what it was all about. He repeated his message four times. Then he put a stop to it all.

Pulled out all the connections, took his rucksack and sidled out. Just as he was about to close the door, the whole exchange started flashing and ringing. It looked as if it were about to explode.

"What the hell...?" he heard Asta exclaim from the back room.

Then he closed the door quietly and tiptoed down the stairs.

He ran all the way home. He was suppressing a loud salvo of laughter. But he waited until he was back in his own kitchen before allowing it to burst out.

His invisible revenge had now pinned down the Caviar Man. And Gertrud had got her own back.

He sat down at the kitchen table and rubbed out all the telephone numbers he'd written on the inside cover of his logbook. Then he returned the book to the showcase featuring the *Celestine*.

He felt tired. Or perhaps it was a feeling of relief. Like when a stomachache passes over.

He had put things right.

It was all over, at long last.

Now he would be able to turn his attention to all the other important things. Finishing the geography game. Finding a good friend. A best friend. Going with Simon Windstorm to Four Winds Lake.

Gertrud would be back to normal.

The Miracle wouldn't worry him anymore.

When his twelfth birthday came round, he might well have forgotten all about everything.

Blasted the Ljusdal bus out of his mind...

He took a few more spoonfuls of jam. One of the jars was nearly empty. But he'd earned it.

He felt a bit sorry for Asta Bagge.

But only a little bit. After all, she'd helped somebody to do a good deed.

She might even believe that it was a Miracle?

That it really was the Lord of the Night who had called all twelve telephone numbers, then disappeared without a trace....

— TWELVE —

The next evening Joel followed the tracks left by the Black Panther.

It was a Shadow Beast that only Joel knew about.

. The Black Panther lived in a cave under the railway bridge. Whenever a train went rattling over the bridge, you could hear the beast roar. . . .

The day after Joel's revenge on the Caviar Man he was the most attentive pupil in the whole class. Only once, when he remembered that Miss Nederström might have climbed over the fence while wearing her wooly long johns under her long skirt, did he start giggling. A storm of laughter was brewing up inside him, but Miss Nederström gave him a stern look before it broke out.

Joel did everything he could to be like all the others. He didn't want to be noticed. He didn't want to be a

Miracle Man. Now he just wanted to be an ordinary pupil.

He had dinner with Sara in the evening. Trying hard to make it sound like no more than an offhand question, he asked what the beer drinkers in the bar had been talking about that day.

"Huh, I don't listen to their chatter," said Sara. "I'd get an earache if I did. It's bad enough having aching feet after all that running around."

"But there must have been something they were all talking about," Joel insisted. He wanted to know.

And he got to know.

"Apparently there was some idiot phoning lots of people in the middle of the night and waking them up," said Sara. "Nobody seems to know who did it, or how. But I suspect it was Asta at the Telegraph Office who'd drunk a bit too much port wine."

Joel could feel himself blushing. So he hadn't been dreaming after all! He really had been in the Telegraph Office during the night!

"That sounds odd," he said casually, chewing a piece of veal chop.

"Asta only talks," said Sara. "There's nothing odd about that...."

Joel felt in very high spirits when he walked home. Now at last he could be normal again. He sat down at the kitchen table and wrote in the inside cover of his logbook:

"The Secret Society Lords of the Underworld has completed its mission. The Caviar Man has been defeated."

That meant that the book was completely full.

He would have to buy a new logbook. He'd be able to write in it about all the things that hadn't happened yet!

I'll soon be twelve, he thought as he stood in front of the cracked shaving mirror. Then there'll only be three more years before I'm fifteen.

He thought he looked older. Older than the day before. His eyes weren't quite so staring. His hair wasn't quite as tousled.

"I've been in the Underworld," he said to the mirror. "I've defeated the Caviar Man."

Then he rushed off to Gertrud's house. As he raced over the bridge like a railway engine, the Black Panther didn't dare to roar. Who dares to roar at a man who has defeated the Caviar Man?

He paused to get his breath back when he came to Gertrud's gate.

Now he would tell her everything. The whole story from start to finish. And he wasn't frightened in the least. Gertrud would understand. She'd be bound to have a good laugh once she understood what it was all about. But she would be impressed by what he had done at the Telegraph Office.

Joel didn't doubt for a moment. Gertrud was like that.

He looked up at the sky. Stars were twinkling like

thousands of cats' eyes. He almost felt dizzy at the thought of how many stars there were.

Could it really be true? That there are more stars than there are ants in an anthill?

It felt very special, almost solemn, that cold September night. The month would soon be over. It would never come back. Then it would be October, and the first heavy snow would start to fall.

Before it melted he would be twelve. Twelve years old. He had lived a whole clockface of years.

It felt strange. Solemn. As if he had almost caught up with the future . . .

He could hear Simon Windstorm's lorry in the distance.

Then he went through the gate, through the door and told the whole story to Gertrud. . . .